Books by Trevor Forest

Faylinn Frost and the Snow Fairies

Abigail Pink's Angel

Peggy Larkin's War

The Wishnotist

Stanley Stickle Hates Homework

Stanley Stickle Does Not Have A Girlfriend

Magic Molly (book one) The Mirror Maze

Magic Molly (book two) Gloop

Magic Molly (book three) The Yellow Eye

Magic Molly Christmas Carole (Christmas Special)

Magic Molly (book four) The Fire Witch

Magic Molly Halloween Hattie (Halloween Special)

http://www.trevorforest.com
http://www.trevorbelshaw.com

Peggy Larkin's War

by

Trevor Forest

The Thank You Bit.

I'd like to express my eternal gratitude to all the people who assisted me in this venture. Without them this book simply wouldn't be here.

Special thanks to Maureen Vincent-Northam and David Robinson for their expert advice and editing skills. Marit Meredith for her support, encouragement and for finding me the wonderful artist, Marie Fullerton.

Extra special thanks to my two Springer Spaniels, Molly and Maisie, for keeping me company and for not being too noisy during the writing process.

PEGGY LARKIN'S WAR

CHAPTER ONE

The steam engine hissed as the station guard checked his watch, puffed out his cheeks and blew on his whistle. 'Evacuation Express Number Three will leave in five minutes,' he announced.

All along the platform, hundreds of mothers, grandparents and a few fathers, hugged their children and said their goodbyes. The train blew thick grey smoke from its chimney and seemed impatient to set off.

Peggy Larkin stood forlornly while her mother and grandmother checked that she had everything she needed for the journey. Her brother, Harry, fidgeted excitedly, eager to get onto the train.

Mrs Larkin slipped the strap of the gas mask over Peggy's head and checked that her label was in place on the lapel of her coat.

'I feel like a piece of luggage with this label on,' moaned Peggy.

'Your new family will want to know who you are and where you are from, dear,' Mrs Larkin explained.

'They only have to ask me, Mum, I'll tell them what they want to know.'

Mrs Larkin smiled fondly at her daughter. 'It's the rules, Peg, I didn't make them, Mr Churchill did.'

'Well, they're stupid rules,' said Peggy.

Mrs Larkin hugged her daughter again, then stepped back as a tear ran down her cheek. She wiped it away with the back of her hand. 'Something in my eye,' she said.

'I don't want to go, Mum.'

'It's for the best, Peggy. The bombs will start falling here soon. You'll be safer in the country.'

'But you won't be safe, you'll be here, all on your own,' said Peggy.

'I have Grandma and Granddad, dear, I won't be on my own all the time,' Mrs Larkin reassured her.

'Come with us, Mum. There's room on the train, you can share my sandwiches.'

'I have my job, Peggy; I can't just leave like that. Now, give me a smile, when Mr Churchill has sorted out these Nazis, I'll come and fetch you back, Dad will come home from the war and everything will be the same as it ever was.'

Peggy tried another tack. 'What if the family I go to are horrible?'

'Don' t worry about that, Peggy, I sent a letter to Mr Churchill asking him to place you with the nicest family he can find, and you've got Harry with you remember? He'll look after you.'

'I'll miss you, Mum.' Peggy began to cry.

'Don't cry Peg, you'll start me off. Now, where's Harry?'

Harry stuck his head out of the grimy carriage window. 'Come on, Peggy, I've got us a window seat.'

'All aboard,' shouted the guard.

Mrs Appleton, Peggy's teacher, clapped her hands as she marched back and forth along the carriages urging children to get onto the train. 'Come along, everyone on the train. Beth Wilkins, hurry now... St Peter's School pupils, in carriage numbers five to nine, hurry along now.'

Peggy made a lunge for her mother and held on to her coat. 'Please, Mum, plea...'

'Margaret Larkin, get onto the train this minute,' said Mrs Appleton.

Peggy turned towards her teacher and stuck out her jaw.

'I'm not going.'

Grandma Fraser bent down to talk to her granddaughter. She took hold of Peggy's hands and smiled softly.

'Peggy, darling, don't make a scene, please sweetheart? It's hard enough for your mum as it is. Wave to her from the window as you pull away, pretend to be happy, just for me.'

Peggy picked up her little suitcase and the paper carrier bag containing her sandwiches for the journey and stepped onto the train. Harry stood on his seat and shouted out of the window to his grandfather.

'See you soon, Granddad.'

Peggy pushed her case under her seat and stood by the window. The guard blew his whistle and the train began to chug slowly along the track. Peggy's mum and grandparents waved with fixed smiles on their faces. Harry hung out of the window and waved frantically.

'Write as soon as you're settled,' called Mrs Larkin. 'I'll come to visit as soon as I can.'

Peggy forced a smile and gave a small wave. As the train reached the end of the platform it began to turn around a bend. Peggy held her hand higher and waved harder as the tears streamed down her cheeks.

'I don't want to go, Mum,' she cried.

CHAPTER TWO

After an hour they began to leave the built-up areas behind and the houses became fewer and further apart. Peggy looked dejectedly out of the window and refused to join in with the quiz that the teacher was holding. Harry sat quietly reading the comic his grandfather had given to him at the station. He looked up as he turned a page.

'Cheer up, Peggy. We're going on holiday.'

Peggy looked glum. 'Some holiday. No beach, no sea, no Mum and Dad.'

'It might be like school camp,' said Harry, optimistically. 'There were lots of things to do when we were there.'

'We were only there a week,' said Peggy. 'We could be away for years this time.'

An hour further on, the scenery had changed completely. Peggy had never seen so many trees in her life, there were far more trees than houses. Occasionally the train rattled past the edge of a sleepy, thatched-roofed village, but mainly the view was of green fields and rolling hills. Peggy had never been out of the city before and found all the wide-open spaces a little disconcerting. Mrs Appleton began an impromptu nature lesson, pointing out different types of trees while some of the younger children tried to count the cows and sheep that littered the fields in the distance.

The train passed through dozens of small stations without stopping. Peggy looked for a sign on the platforms to try to get a clue as to their whereabouts, but they had all been removed.

'How are we supposed to work out where we are?' she complained.

'All road signs and station names have been removed to confuse the Germans if they invade,' explained Mrs Appleton. 'Their soldiers won't be able to work out where they are.'

'But it will confuse our soldiers too,' argued Peggy. 'They won't be able to find the Germans because they won't know where they are either.'

'They'll have maps, Peggy.'

'The Germans might have maps too, and ...'

'They won't,' said the teacher, firmly. 'Don't argue.'

Peggy stuck out her bottom lip and went back to looking for clues to where they were.

'Stupid rules,' she muttered under her breath.

Eventually the excited atmosphere in the carriage began to wane and one or two of the younger children demanded to be taken home. Mrs Appleton started a game of 'I spy', but there wasn't the enthusiasm to continue it for long. The teacher then got them to sing *'Ten Green Bottles'* and *'Wish Me Luck as You Wave Me Goodbye,'* to brighten the mood.

At noon they opened their first pack of sandwiches and Mrs Appleton handed out small bottles of milk which they drank through waxed paper straws. After lunch the teacher walked to the end of the carriage and clapped for silence.

'In an hour or so we will arrive at our destination. There will be volunteer families waiting who have kindly offered to take us in and keep us safe for our mums and dads back home. I expect you all to be on your best behaviour while you are in their charge and never forget that the good name of the school is at stake.'

Mrs Appleton looked around slowly to make sure everyone was paying attention before she continued.

'When you are billeted and settled, the first thing you should do is write a letter home, your parents will want to know that you have arrived safely and you are happy in your new surroundings. Always remember that it is just as hard for your new family to accept a new face as it is for you to accept them. Try your best to fit in with their ways, you are the guest, it is your responsibility to adapt to your new way of life. Now then, shall I sing a song to remind you of better times ahead?'

Mrs Appleton cleared her throat and began to sing.

'We'll meet again ...'

By the time Mrs Appleton reached the second verse, almost every child in the carriage had joined in. Vera Lynn was a popular singer and everyone had heard the song on the wireless, many times.

*****

Thirty minutes later the train pulled into a tiny station. A guard got off and walked to the stationmaster's office. A few minutes later he returned carrying a pile of forms. Mrs Appleton opened the window and spoke to the guard.

'Excuse me. Why have we stopped?'

'We're waiting for Evacuation Express number two to clear the station just along the line, madam,' the guard replied. He moved closer to the window and looked around to make sure he couldn't be overheard. 'That's the end of the line. You'll all get off there.'

Mrs Appleton pulled her head back inside, closed the window and clapped her hands to get attention. 'It seems that we are nearing the end of our journey children. Can you all check your labels and make sure you have everything you brought onto the train with you, don't leave anything behind; you won't be able to get it back later.'

Peggy realised that she needed to use the lavatory urgently. She walked down to the toilet in the next carriage and found a queue of about ten girls. One was banging on the lavatory door.

'Hurry up, Constance, there's a queue a mile long out here.'

'I'm sick, leave me alone,' came the muffled reply.

Peggy looked out onto the empty platform and saw a sign pointing the way to the public toilets. She thought about going back to ask Mrs Appleton's permission to leave the train but she couldn't wait any longer.

'Surely no one would mind if I use the station toilets,' she said to herself.

Peggy dropped the handle on the door and jumped down onto the platform. The guard was in a conversation with a teacher at a window further down the track.

Peggy followed the arrow and found her way to the conveniences. Two minutes later, much-relieved, Peggy ran the single cold water tap and washed her hands. As she reached for the towel she heard the guards whistle and the chug of the engine.

'Oh no!' cried Peggy. 'Wait for me.'

Peggy raced outside just in time to see the train pull away. She ran after it waving her hands in the air.

'Stop, please...'

Peggy stood at the end of the platform and watched in horror as the train disappeared into the distance. 'Please stop,' she whispered again.

Peggy felt a tear run down her cheek and for the third time that day she began to cry.

CHAPTER THREE

'Hello, what's this? Do I have a misplaced child on my platform?'

Peggy turned to find a fat man with red cheeks and a friendly smile looking down at her. He wore a dark blue uniform and a peaked cap with a red band. He had a pair of round spectacles perched on the end of his nose.

'I missed my train,' sobbed Peggy.

'Only the special trains are stopping here today,' said the man. 'If you're from the village then I'm sorry but local trains won't resume until next week.'

'I'm not from the village, I'm from London... My name is Peggy Larkin and I needed to go to the lavatory but there was a queue and I saw the sign and thought I might use the one on the platform but the train went and I got left behind.'

'Oh dear, it seems you have been a little unfortunate, Peggy Larkin. Dry your eyes now and come with me to my office, we'll put the kettle on and see what's to be done, shall we?'

Peggy wiped her eyes on her sleeve and sniffed. 'Can't you just send me back to London?'

The man shook his head. 'I don't think I can do that, but I do have a telephone in the office and I can ring ahead to let them know that they're one short.'

'I'd rather go home,' said Peggy.

The man smiled and squatted down in front of her. 'I'm sure you'll be happy up the road there, just give it a chance, Peggy. It really isn't going to be safe in London for a good while yet. I'm Mr Hobson by the way. I'm the stationmaster.'

Mr Hobson filled his kettle and placed it on a gas hob, then he rinsed out the teapot and put in three spoons of tea from a small tin. 'Nothing like a cup of tea to settle the nerves,' he said.

The stationmaster winked and looked around as if checking to see if anyone was listening. 'I've got a bit of sugar hidden away in my cupboard, would you like some in your tea?'

Peggy nodded, she liked sweet tea.

Mr Hobson dropped two lumps into Peggy's cup and three into his own. He winked at her again. 'I've got a sweet tooth,' he confided.

'My grandma has too,' said Peggy, beginning to feel a little better about things.

Peggy looked around the office while Mr Hobson tended to the whistling kettle. There was a telephone on the desk alongside two trays, one marked In and one marked Out. In front of the stationmaster's chair was a large blotting pad on which lay a black and silver fountain pen. On the walls the familiar government posters warned that, *'walls have ears,'* and *'careless talk costs lives,'* another advised people to, *'dig for victory.'*

Mr Hobson poured the tea, settled back in his chair and took a noisy sip.

'Ah, that's hit the spot.'

Peggy sipped at her tea and nodded in agreement.

Mr Hobson took a white form from a drawer and picked up his pen. 'Better get the report done, Peggy. Shall we go over it again?'

Peggy told Mr Hobson everything that had happened to her so far; the stationmaster made careful notes.

'I take it your brother is still on the train, Peggy?'

'So are my suitcase and sandwiches,' said Peggy.

'Right,' said Mr Hobson. 'I'll ring Middle Markham station and let them know you're here.'

'Middle Markham, is that where I'm going?' asked Peggy.

'Oops, I shouldn't have told you that,' said Mr Hobson. 'It's supposed to be a secret.' He cleaned his spectacles on his tie, placed them back on his nose and looked over them at Peggy. 'Not to worry, you don't look like a German spy to me, so no harm done.'

Mr Hobson rang the stationmaster at Middle Markham and jotted down a number on his blotter. After a few minutes he finished his conversation, put down the phone then picked it up again and dialled the number he had been given.

'Hello, this is the stationmaster at Lower Markham. I believe I have one of your evacuees here, there was a bit of a mix up and she got left behind.'

Mr Hobson listened for a while and nodded his head once or twice. 'Right, I'll see she gets on Evacuation Express number four, it should be here in a few minutes. Can someone pick her up from Middle Markham station?'

He looked across to Peggy and winked. 'That's put the cat among the pigeons,' he said.

Mr Hobson began to get a little impatient with whoever he was talking to. He rolled his eyes once or twice and drummed his fingers on the desk.

'I see, well I can't bring her to you myself so someone will have to meet her there...Right, Mrs Henderson will pick her up and take her to the reception centre at Middle Markham. That's good. The people on the next train are headed for Upper Markham. I have no idea how they are going to get them there, they don't have a station.'

Mr Hobson put the phone down and smiled at Peggy.

'We seem to have it all sorted, Peggy. We are going to put you on the next train which will take you to Middle Markham. When you get off you are to go straight to the stationmaster's office. He is expecting you. A lady called Mrs Henderson will pick you up from there; you should be with your brother again by this evening if it all goes to plan.'

Peggy thanked Mr Hobson and asked to use the lavatory again. By the time she got back to the platform the train was pulling in to the station.

CHAPTER FOUR

Mr Hobson had a quick word with the guard from Evacuation Express number four and Peggy was allowed to get onto the train. There were no spare seats so she stood by the door where she could look out of the window. Mr Hobson waved to her from his office doorway.

The train pulled away from Lower Markham station half an hour later and chugged slowly up the two-mile length of track that led to Middle Markham. Because she was right by the door Peggy was first off the train. She looked for the sign for the stationmaster's office but couldn't find one, so she knocked on the ticket office door instead.

The door opened and Peggy found herself looking at a thin-faced man wearing a uniform identical to Mr Hobson's.

'Yes?' he barked.

'I'm Peggy Larkin,' said Peggy.

It was obvious from his face that the name hadn't registered. Peggy put her hand to her mouth and whispered. 'I'm from Lower Markham...'

The man looked confused. 'You shouldn't have been able to get onto that train at Lower Markham, it's for evacuees only.'

'I am an evacuee,' said Peggy.

'Why do you need evacuating from Lower Markham?' asked the man. 'It's only two miles away from here.'

'I didn't need evacuating from Lower Markham,' said Peggy. 'I was only there for a couple of hours.'

The man took off his cap and scratched his head. 'But you said you were an evacuee...'

'I am,' said Peggy patiently. 'I'm from London.'

'You just said you were from Lower Markham...'

Peggy began to get confused herself. She took a deep breath and explained.

'I've been sent from Lower Markham by Mr Hobson, I got off the train to use the lavatory and it went without me. He telephoned about an hour ago; he said I was to report to the stationmaster.'

'I see,' said the man. 'You want Mr Wright then, he's just gone home for his tea. He'll be back in about an hour.'

Peggy sighed and looked at her shoes. 'Where shall I wait?'

The ticket master pointed to a bench on the platform. It was already taken by a group of teachers from the train. Peggy sighed again and wandered across to the bench seat. There seemed nothing else to do but wait, so she sat on the floor and closed her eyes.

She was woken by a woman's voice and a hand shaking her shoulder.

'Come on, dear, wake up, they'll be leaving in a minute.'

Peggy looked around the empty platform. 'Where did everyone go?'

'They're all lined up on the lane behind the station ready to march up to Upper Markham. Hurry up, you'll be left behind.'

'I've already been left behind,' said Peggy. 'Are you Mrs Henderson?'

'No, dear, I'm Mrs Partridge. I'm the cleaner.'

'I'm not with that lot,' said Peggy nodding towards the exit. 'I was on the earlier train, but I got off and it went without me, so they've sent me here to wait for Mrs Henderson.'

Mrs Partridge put down her mop and bucket. 'Beryl Henderson, from the big house?'

'I don't know,' said Peggy. 'I was told to find the station master and wait for her, but he's gone home for his tea.'

'He's back now. That's his office over there.'

Mrs Partridge pointed to a plain green door next to the ticket office. Peggy thanked her and hurried down the platform. She knocked on the door and waited, there was no answer so she knocked again.

A tall, broad shouldered man with a moustache opened the door. His uniform didn't fit properly, his trouser legs stopped well above his ankles and his jacket was pulled tight across the front.

'I heard you the first time,' he said.

'Sorry,' said Peggy. 'I thought...'

'Don't think, wait,' said the man. 'Didn't they teach you any manners at home?'

'Yes but...'

'No buts, just stand there and wait until I ask you to come in.'

The man slammed the door in Peggy's face. She heard the clomping of feet and a chair being dragged back. A minute later he called for her to enter.

Peggy walked over to the front of the desk and stood quietly. The stationmaster flicked through some papers, signed one at the bottom, then leant back in his chair and glared at her.

'Do you know how much trouble you've caused?'

'I'm sorry, I needed to go...'

'I don't suppose you gave a thought for anyone else,' he continued.

'I thought I had enough time but...'

'Thinking isn't really your strong point is it?' growled the stationmaster.

Peggy remained silent. There didn't seem much point in saying anything if he wasn't going to listen.

'What's wrong now,' he said. 'Cat got your tongue?'

'No.'

'No, sir,' snapped the stationmaster.

'No, sir,' repeated Peggy.

'That's better.' Mr Wright leaned across his desk and studied Peggy's label. 'Larkin, from London.' He checked the form on his desk, filled in a few more details, then signed the bottom with a flourish. 'Do you know how to make tea?'

'Yes, sir, I make it for Mum on Sundays.'

The stationmaster looked a little less angry. 'From now on you may address me as Mr Wright.' He pointed to a kettle, then across to a dirty looking sink. 'Kettle there, water there, the tea is in the silver tin and the milk is in the cupboard below the sink.'

Mr Wright watched as Peggy filled the kettle, then went back to his paperwork. Peggy made the tea and carried the cup and saucer over to his desk. He sniffed at it suspiciously before taking a sip.

'Not bad, for a Londoner.'

The telephone rang as he was drinking the tea. Mr Wright rolled his eyes then snatched it from the cradle. 'Stationmaster...Yes she's here, being a nuisance, getting in the way.'

'I really hope you don't have children at home,' muttered Peggy.

Mr Wright scowled at Peggy, took the phone from his ear and put his hand over the mouthpiece. 'Speak when you're spoken to,' he hissed.

Peggy bit her lip and looked at her shoes as the stationmaster put the phone to his ear again. 'Very well, if that's the best you can do,' he barked.

Mr Wright slammed the phone down and glared at Peggy. 'It appears that they are having a few problems at the reception centre. Mrs Henderson will be over to pick you up in about twenty minutes. Take your suitcase and wait outside.'

Peggy looked to where Mr Wright was pointing and found her case under the window.

'Did they leave my sandwiches too, I'm hungry?'

Mr Wright looked at the grease-proofed paper lying in his waste bin and licked his lips. 'I confiscated those. Now go and wait outside.'

Peggy put her case down on the platform and sat on the bench, her tummy was rumbling and she was thirsty. Mrs Partridge appeared with her mop and bucket.

'Hello again, why so glum?'

'I'm hungry and Mr Wright ate all my sandwiches,' said Peggy.

'Did he indeed,' said Mrs Partridge. 'Hang on there, I'll be back in a minute.'

Mrs Partridge disappeared into the cleaner's room and came back with a thick slice of bread, a lump of cheese and a small cup of milk. 'Here you are, dear, you can have my supper, I'm not really hungry.'

'No, I couldn't take...'

'You eat it up, dear, I can get mine when I get home.' Mrs Partridge winked, picked up her mop and bucket and headed for Mr Wrights office. 'Good luck, dear, I hope you enjoy your stay.'

*****

Mrs Henderson was a trim looking woman who wore a tweed suit and brown shoes with silver buckles, her hair was pulled into a tight bun. She arrived pushing her bicycle.

'Are you the Larkin girl?' she asked.

'Yes, Miss,' replied Peggy.

'Wait there while I sign your release form.'

Mrs Henderson leaned her bicycle against the wall and walked into Mr Wright's office. Two minutes later she was back with a brown envelope in her hands.

'Right then, Margaret, let's be off.'

'It's Peggy,' said Peggy.

Mrs Henderson tutted. 'It says Margaret on your label and it says Margaret on your form, so Margaret, it is.'

'No one calls me Margaret,' muttered Peggy under her breath.

'Then it's high time someone did, seeing as it's your proper name,' said Mrs Henderson.

Peggy was amazed that she had been heard, she was glad she hadn't called her a rude name.

Mrs Henderson wheeled her bicycle along the station platform, then turned to the left and led Peggy at a brisk pace along a leafy country lane. Peggy's case was only small but after a while it began to feel like it was made of lead and she soon found herself lagging behind. Mrs Henderson stopped until Peggy caught up, then set off again at exactly the same pace.

After a while the trees began to thin out and were replaced by rows of small thatched cottages with low stone walls in front of nicely kept gardens. A few people stood on their doorsteps chatting while they caught the final rays of the early autumn sun.

'Found your stray have you, Beryl?' called a woman.

'She looks like she needs feeding up, poor mite,' called another.

A few yards further on they came to a wooden building with a short set of steps leading up to the entrance. On the door was a sign that read, 'Village Hall, please wipe your feet.'

Mrs Henderson parked up her bike and opened the door. Peggy wiped her feet on the coconut mat and followed her inside.

The room looked bigger from the inside than it had from the street. At one end was a low stage that took up the full width of the room. On the stage, in front of a piano, sat a woman wearing curlers and a headscarf.

'Ah, you found her then?'

Mrs Henderson looked around the hall with a puzzled look on her face. 'Where's Emily Thompson? She's down to take this girl.'

'She's been and gone,' said the woman. 'She told me to give you a message. It seems her sister has come down from Nottingham, she's here for the duration so she doesn't have room for this one now.'

'Bother.' Mrs Henderson brought her hand down on the table with a thud.

'Where's Harry?' asked Peggy. 'I'm supposed to go with him.'

The woman closed the lid over the piano keys and got to her feet. 'If he's a short boy with fair hair then Emily took him, but she doesn't have room for two now, her sister has...'

'Yes, yes, we heard you the first time, Harriet,' said Mrs Henderson. 'The thing is, what are we going to do with young Margaret here?'

Peggy felt tears welling up again. 'I'm supposed to go with Harry.'

'You'll have to take her, Beryl,' said Harriet. 'You've got a big enough house, you could fit a dozen kids in there.'

'I didn't volunteer,' said Mrs Henderson. 'I offered to help organise, I didn't offer to take anyone in.'

'Well she's got to go somewhere, poor little thing.'

'I'm well aware of that, Harriet, do you have any room?'

Harriet shook her head. 'You know I live with my old mum and dad, Beryl. I have to sleep on a camp bed in the living room, so there's no room at our house.'

Mrs Henderson came to a decision. She turned to Peggy with a look of frustration.

'Very well,' she sighed. 'But it's only for tonight; we'll have to find someone permanent tomorrow.'

CHAPTER FIVE

Mrs Henderson picked up a large pile of forms, stuffed them into a canvas bag, then set about checking Peggy's head for lice.

'No nits, thank goodness,' she said. 'Remind me to congratulate your mother if ever I meet her.'

Mrs Henderson left Harriet to lock up, grabbed her bicycle and set off at a pace through the village. Peggy trotted along behind with her case. After a mile or so, Peggy found herself lagging seriously behind. Eventually Mrs Henderson noticed and rode back to where Peggy had stopped to catch her breath.

'You're not very fit for a young girl are you, Margaret Larkin?'

'It's my case, Miss,' said Peggy.

'It's only a small one,' Mrs Henderson scoffed. 'Come along, it will be dark soon.'

Mrs Henderson stood to the side of the narrow lane as she heard the sound of hooves. Two minutes later a horse and cart packed with hay bales appeared from around the bend. The driver called to Mrs Henderson.

'Hello there, Mrs Henderson, have you been lumbered too?'

'Hello, Mr Brown. If you mean young Margaret here, then yes, but I assure you it's only for the one night.'

'I've had Alf for a week now,' said the cart driver. 'He's a cheeky monkey.'

'They all are,' said Mrs Henderson. 'I don't' know what they teach them in London but manners seem to be well down the list.'

Peggy bit her tongue as the two adults talked about her as though she couldn't hear.

'This one's clean at least,' said Mrs Henderson. 'Some of them are infested with lice.'

'I had to shave Alf's head before my wife would let him in the house,' said the man.

Peggy pulled up a handful of grass from the verge and fed it to the horse. She stroked his nose as he ate it.

'Can I offer you a lift?' asked Mr Brown.

'That's very kind of you,' said Mrs Henderson. 'It will take us all night to get home at this rate.'

'It's not a problem; I have to pass by your place to get home anyway.'

The farmer took the bicycle and lifted it onto the cart, then helped Mrs Henderson into the passenger seat. Finally he turned to Peggy.

'Up you get.'

Peggy climbed onto the back of the cart and perched herself on a bale of hay. Mr Brown passed her the suitcase and jumped up to the driver's seat.

'Thank Mr Brown for his kindness, Margaret.'

Peggy's thank you was left in the air as the cart pulled away.

Peggy leaned back against the hay, closed her eyes and smiled to herself. Riding on the cart beat walking any day of the week. Peggy's legs were aching, she was very active at home but she wasn't used to walking long distances.

Mrs Henderson and Mr Brown chatted about local village matters while Peggy hummed a tune to herself in the back of the cart. She was beginning to like the quiet of the countryside.

Mr Brown seemed to read her thoughts.

'It's a bit different to the city isn't it? You can hear the birds sing out here.'

'I can hear the birds sing at home,' replied Peggy. 'We have blackbirds and sparrows but there are more pigeons that anything else. I've been listening to the bird songs. I'd like to learn which song goes with which bird while I'm here.'

Mr Brown seemed pleased. 'You've got a good one there, Beryl. Maybe you should think about keeping her.'

Mrs Henderson shook her head. 'No thank you. I don't need a child under my feet. I'm far too busy.'

The horse and cart made its leisurely way along the narrow country lanes. Some of them were little more than tracks. At a crossroads Mr Brown ordered the horse to stop with a sharp, 'whoa' and looked around for traffic. Peggy stared back along the long winding lane they had just travelled. It was flanked by tall hedges on both sides. In places there were gaps in the hedgerow where Peggy could see into the trees beyond. Behind the cart a space had been cleared to allow access to the wood. Peggy's eyes followed a narrow path that led into the trees. Suddenly a man's face appeared in the gap. He was unshaven and had a mop of greasy hair that fell across his forehead. His eyes narrowed as he curled back his lip and snarled.

Peggy screamed.

'Whatever is the matter, child?' asked Mrs Henderson.

'There's a face in the hedge,' cried Peggy.

Mr Brown jumped down from his seat to investigate. 'A face you say?'

'In the hedge,' cried Peggy, still shaken.

Mr Brown searched but found no one. 'You're imagining things, my girl, there's no one there.'

'There was,' said Peggy. 'He had a beard and cruel eyes.'

Mr Brown laughed good naturedly. 'I think the country air has got to you, girl. It's very tiring for people who aren't used to it.'

Mr Brown climbed back to his seat, clicked his tongue and shook the reigns. The horse began to walk slowly across the road. Peggy looked back towards the wood, but whoever had been hiding there had gone.

Five minutes later they pulled up in front of a large, red brick house set behind a thick hawthorn hedge. Mr Brown helped Mrs Henderson down and retrieved her bicycle from the cart. Peggy passed him her case, then climbed awkwardly down herself.

Before Mrs Henderson could remind her, Peggy thanked the farmer for the ride. Mr Brown touched his cap with his long fingers. 'You're very welcome, young lady.'

He turned back to Mrs Henderson. 'Send her down for the milk in the morning; you may as well make use of her while she's here.'

Mrs Henderson shook her head. 'She'll only get lost, then I'll have to come and find her. She's good at getting lost.'

*****

Mrs Henderson opened the front door with a long key that she fished out from her bag and led Peggy inside. She found herself in a small, whitewashed room with a couple of shelves on the walls and several pairs of boots and shoes on the floor.

'Shoes off here please. I don't' want your muddy footprints all over my polished floors.'

Peggy undid the straps on her shoes and kicked them off. Mrs Henderson slid off her shoes and slipped her feet into a pair of soft-looking slippers. Peggy eyed them jealously.

Mrs Henderson noticed the look and rummaged around in a cupboard until she found another pair.

'These are my old ones and they'll probably be a little big, but if you can keep them on your feet you're welcome to borrow them.'

Peggy slipped her feet into the fur lined slippers. Luckily Mrs Henderson didn't have very big feet and she was able to keep them on by scrunching her toes up to make them a little tighter.

Mrs Henderson struck a match, lit a paraffin lamp that sat on an oblong table and led Peggy into the kitchen.

Peggy noticed that there were electric light switches on the walls. Mrs Henderson seemed to sense Peggy's forthcoming question.

'I don't use the electric lights, not while the blackout is on.'

'Never?' asked Peggy.

'Never,' said Mrs Henderson firmly. 'One chink of light through the blackout curtains could guide an enemy bomber toward us. There's less chance of him seeing a bit of light from a paraffin lamp; I do use candles too.'

As if to prove the point, Mrs Henderson lit two candles and stuck them onto saucers with hot wax. She placed one on the long wooden kitchen table and the other on the draining board next to the sink.

'Right, to business,' she said.

Peggy followed her from room to room as she pulled the blackout curtains closed. When she had finished she stood at the bottom of a wide staircase and turned to Peggy.

'Make yourself useful, Margaret. Put the kettle on. You'll find matches at the side of the stove. You can make the tea while I sort out a bed for you. I suppose you do know how to make tea?'

Peggy nodded and turned back towards the kitchen. 'I'm getting lots of practice today,' she whispered.

'Good,' called Mrs Henderson. 'I expect it to be perfect then.'

*****

Mrs Henderson reappeared about ten minutes later. Peggy had just put the huge brown teapot on the table.

'It's just like the one we have at home,' she said.

Mrs Henderson produced a beautifully painted china cup and saucer from a cupboard on the wall and placed it carefully on the table, then she opened the cupboard under the sink and pulled out a chipped white cup.

'This will have to do,' she said. 'I'm not going to risk my best china.'

Mrs Henderson poured the tea and added milk from a jug she retrieved from the pantry. Just as Mr Wright had done earlier in the day, she sniffed at it before taking a sip.

Peggy sniffed at her cup too, in case it was a thing country folk did.

'Do you have any sugar?' asked Peggy.

'Don't you know there's a war on?' said Mrs Henderson quickly. 'They'll be rationing it soon, so it's best to get used to doing without.'

Mrs Henderson sipped at the tea again, a smile flashed across her face.

'I have to say I'm surprised and very pleased at the same time, Margaret. This is an excellent cup of tea.'

Mrs Henderson drained her cup and poured another. She took a sip and leaned back in her chair. 'It's been a long day today, an early night is called for I think.' She closed her eyes and was silent for a while. 'Have you eaten?' she asked suddenly.

'I had a bit of bread and cheese at the station, Mrs Part...'

'Good, I had tea at the reception hall. We'll get off to bed after this shall we? We've a busy day ahead of us tomorrow and I want an early start.'

*****

Mrs Henderson picked up the saucer holding the candle and passed it to Peggy.

'Don't go burning the house down will you?' she said.

Peggy promised to be careful and Mrs Henderson led her out to the hallway.

'Wait here.'

Peggy waited while Mrs Henderson locked all the doors and checked the windows, then followed her up the wide carpeted staircase. When they reached the first floor she pointed to the right.

'My bedroom is the second door along that passage should there be an emergency in the night. I've put you in the attic room; you're not scared of creaking noises are you?'

Peggy shook her head. 'I sleep in the attic room at home too.'

Mrs Henderson led her a short distance along the left hand passage. 'This is the bathroom and lavatory. You are not to go beyond this point. The other rooms on this side of the landing are out of bounds, do I make myself clear?' Peggy nodded and Mrs Henderson led her up another flight of stairs to the top of the house.

Peggy's room was larger than she thought it was going to be. There was a chair at the side of a comfortable looking bed for her to put her clothes on and on the floor next to the bed was a small carpet. There was a sink on the wall with a striped towel hanging on a rail underneath. On the sink itself was a small bar of soap and a tin of tooth powder.

'Do you own a toothbrush, Margaret?'

Peggy nodded. 'It's in my case, downstairs.'

'Well, we're not going down there to get it now; I put out all the candles. You'll have to stick your finger in the powder and do it that way for tonight. Once again I have to congratulate your mother. A lot of children don't clean their teeth at all.'

Mrs Henderson walked from the room and began to close the door behind her.

'Goodnight, Mrs Henderson,' said Peggy. 'Thank you for looking after me today.'

Mrs Henderson stopped for a moment, a smile played on her lips. Peggy thought she was going to come back into the room but instead she turned away and closed the door behind her. Peggy was sure she heard a muffled whisper as she went back down the stairs.

'Goodnight, Margaret Larkin.'

CHAPTER SIX

Peggy woke to the sound of Mrs Henderson's voice. It was just getting light so she had opened the blackout shutters.

'It's time you were up and about, Margaret Larkin. It's almost five thirty.'

Peggy was horrified.

'Five thir...'

'We don't spend all day in bed like you city folk,' said Mrs Henderson. 'Come on now, get washed and dressed, I've brought your case up.'

Peggy went to the bathroom and had a strip wash, then she got some clean underwear and a print dress from her case. She tucked her old clothes under her arm and went down to the kitchen. Mrs Henderson was at the table drinking tea.

'Could I borrow a paper bag to put my dirty clothes in please?'

Mrs Henderson took the clothes from Peggy and dropped them in a basket by the door.

'I'll be washing my own clothes later on; I'll put yours in with mine and deliver them on to wherever it is you end up.'

Peggy sat at the table and poured herself a cup of tea. Bubbling away on the stove was a pot of porridge, Mrs Henderson splashed two ladles full into a bowl and placed it in front of Peggy.

'Porridge, a good start to the day.'

Peggy was about to ask if it had any sugar in it, but stopped herself just in time. Mrs Henderson opened the cupboard and pulled out a tin of golden syrup.

'One spoonful only, my girl.'

Peggy dipped her spoon into the tin and rolled it around so that it collected as much of the sticky, gold coloured goo as possible, then she mixed it into her porridge and ate it with relish. Afterwards she washed her bowl and cup in the sink as Mrs Henderson looked on.

'Once again, I have to give great credit to your mother, Margaret Larkin. She has obviously tried very hard with you.'

'I have chores to do at home,' said Peggy. 'I run errands and I have to wash up twice a week after tea. I always have to wash up my own breakfast bowl.'

'That's exactly how it should be,' said Mrs Henderson. 'You used it after all.'

At nine o'clock, Mrs Henderson locked the door behind her and led Peggy out into the lane.

'I won't use my bicycle today, we can catch the bus,' she said.

As they walked to the bus stop, Peggy told Mrs Henderson about the big red double-decker buses they had in London. Mrs Henderson seemed quite impressed but doubted they would be much use in country areas.

'They would never get up and down the lanes round here,' she said.

Peggy agreed.

The bus arrived on time and Peggy and Mrs Henderson took their seats before a conductor asked for their money and issued them with tickets. They got off the bus at the terminus and Mrs Henderson led Peggy along Market Street to the town hall. Just before they went through the imposing front door, she took Peggy to one side and issued a warning.

'I expect you to be on your best behaviour, Margaret. We need to get you sorted out with a new family today so mind your P's and Q's.

'What's a P and Q?' asked Peggy with a puzzled look. She had heard the expression before but had never learned what it meant.

'It means mind your manners,' said Mrs Henderson. 'In we go.'

She led Peggy though the giant hall and up two sets of steps before they walked down a long corridor with doors on both sides. At the bottom of the corridor was a door marked, 'Evacuee Committee.'

Mrs Henderson rapped on the door and pushed it open without waiting for an invitation to enter. At the desk by the window sat an elderly woman with steel-grey hair and thick spectacles.

'Ah, Mrs Henderson. How did it go yesterday?' she asked.

'Mostly very well, apart from young Margaret Larkin here,' said Mrs Henderson.

'Did no one want her? Is there something that we didn't know about?' The clerk studied Peggy through her thick spectacles. 'She looks all right to me.'

Mrs Henderson explained what had gone wrong the previous afternoon. 'The person who should have taken her can no longer take her as she needs the space for a visiting relative.'

'Is there no one else?' asked the clerk.

Mrs Henderson shook her head. 'Apparently not, which is why I've bought her here to see if you can find her a place.'

Mrs Henderson took the pile of placement forms from her canvas bag and handed them to the clerk. 'These are the successful placements. We just need to find somewhere for young Margaret.'

'She has to go to Middle Markham,' said the clerk. 'I have her form here, in triplicate.'

'Can't we put her at Upper Markham with the last intake?' asked Mrs Henderson.

The clerk looked shocked. 'No, she's down to go to the Middle Markham School. All the paperwork's been done; it would cause a lot of bother if we had to change things at this stage. We've got quota's you see?'

Mrs Henderson gave in. She knew better than to try to argue with people in authority. 'Right, I'd better take her back to Middle Markham and ask around again.'

'Can't you take her? ' asked the clerk. 'You have a huge house and you're rattling about in it on your own.'

'No,' said Mrs Henderson quickly. 'I don't want a child in my house, it's...never mind, I just don't want one.'

She led Peggy back out of the town hall and they retraced their steps to the bus terminus. They travelled back to Middle Markham in silence. Peggy began to feel like a piece of luggage again.

At the village hall Mrs Henderson picked up the telephone and rang the village doctor, then the local policeman. She explained the situation and asked if they knew of anyone who would take Peggy. Both said that they couldn't think of anyone.

Mrs Henderson and Harriet worked their way through the parish electoral register looking for people they thought might offer a home to Peggy, but the only names that came up had already taken someone. After an hour Harriet closed the book, sat back and sighed.

'There is no one, we just have to accept it.'

Before Mrs Henderson could reply there was a knock on the door. Harriet opened it to find Sam Fettle standing in the doorway. His clothes were filthy, he had a hole in his jacket and his trousers were held up with a length of string. He stepped inside without wiping his muddy boots on the mat.

'I hear you've got an evacuee going spare,' he growled.

'No one that would suit you, Mr Fettle,' said Harriet.

'I'm not fussy, I just need a hand around the farm,' said Sam.

Mrs Henderson shook her head. 'You mean you need someone to do all the work on your farm while you spend your time in the Dog and Duck.'

'What I do with my time is my own business,' said Sam. 'Now, bring the form here and I'll sign it.' He looked Peggy up and down. 'Is this the one? She doesn't look like she could lift a bucket of slops let alone a sack of potatoes. Still, beggars can't be choosers.'

Mrs Henderson put the electoral register away and slipped the forms into a drawer. 'She's too young for work, Sam, especially the kind of work you need doing. She's never seen a farm before, she wouldn't have a clue how to go about milking or mucking out.'

Sam wasn't about to be put off. 'I hear she has a brother, I'll take them both.'

'Her brother has been placed already, Sam,' said Mrs Henderson. 'Margaret is the only one left.'

Peggy ran behind Harriet and grabbed hold of her skirt. 'Don't let him take me, please... Put me in a children's home, anything, but don't make me go with him.'

Sam scratched at his head with dirty fingernails and took a step forward. 'Come along, Missy, I'm not too bad when you get to know me.'

'It's out of the question, Sam,' said Harriet.

Sam took another step forward. Peggy could smell him from six feet away. 'Where's the form,' he said. 'I'll sign it now. You know I have the right to her if I want her, you can't refuse a volunteer.'

Mrs Henderson took a form from the drawer, unscrewed the top of her fountain pen and began to fill in the form. 'You are quite right, Sam,' she muttered.

Sam scratched under his arm, then had another go at his hair. 'You'll be just fine with me, Missy,' he said.

Peggy backed away towards the far wall, she could not believe what was happening to her. 'Please,' she said, 'Please...'

Mrs Henderson stood up, screwed the top back onto her pen and picked up the form from the desk. 'I'm sorry, Mr Fettle, but I'm afraid Miss Larkin is no longer available.'

'What?'

Mrs Henderson held up the form so that Sam could read it. 'Margaret Larkin has been placed, with me as it turns out.'

Peggy ran to Mrs Henderson and threw her arms around her waist. 'Thank you, thank you...'

Mr Fettle began to argue then realised there was very little he could do about it. He gave Peggy a dirty look and stormed out of the room. Harriet held her nose and went to find a mop and bucket.

'I'll wash the floor with disinfectant, the whole place stinks.'

At four o'clock Mrs Henderson and Peggy began the long walk home. On the way Peggy's new guardian laid out the ground rules.

'It will be your job to lay the fire in the mornings, you will help with the laundry, help keep the place tidy and you will run errands for me. You will make your own bed and you will steer clear of the out of bounds area of the house. You don't have to start school for another week yet so you have plenty of time to settle in and learn how to do your new chores.'

Peggy agreed to everything, she was just pleased not to be going home with Sam Fettle. They walked in silence for a while, then Peggy stopped and tugged at Mrs Henderson's sleeve.

'I know you didn't really want me to live with you, but I promise not to cause any trouble. I'll do my chores and I'll be good.'

Mrs Henderson lifted her hand to stroke Peggy's hair, then took it quickly away. 'I'll get used to the idea I suppose. Now, let's get a move on. You have a letter to write to your mother.'

CHAPTER SEVEN

Peggy took her time composing the letter home. A part of her wanted to tell her mother everything that had happened to her, but another part wanted to hide it away so that she wouldn't worry too much.

Dear Mum,

I miss you, and Grandma and Granddad, and Dad of course.

I've been placed with a nice lady called Mrs Henderson, there is just the two of us in a big house with lots of bedrooms; I'm in the attic room. It has an indoor lavatory and a real bath. We have electricity, but we don't have the lights on because of the blackout.

I'm not with Harry, they had to split us up, he's gone to a nice family in a village a few miles away. Mrs Henderson says she'll take me over to see him soon.

I love the countryside, Mum. It's so peaceful and quiet, there is a bus service but they don't run past the houses like they do at home, we had to walk a mile to get to the bus stop yesterday.

I don't start school until next week, so I'm going to have a look around and get to know the village. One of my chores is to get fresh milk from the farm. I have to do that in the morning before I lay the fire. We get up very early in the country. I was up at five thirty this morning. I'm getting a bit tired now, but I'll get used to it.

We had fish paste sandwiches for tea tonight. I have porridge for breakfast now.

Love you lots, Mum. Write soon, send my love to Dad, Grandma and Granddad.

Love Peggy.

PS. Can you tell Mrs Haggerty, next door, that I don't know what happened to Marjorie. I wasn't there when she was picked.

PPS. I haven't seen any bombers here, I hope you haven't seen any there either.

*****

Peggy folded the letter and slipped it into an envelope. Mrs Henderson looked up from her book at the sound of the paper rustling.

'Don't seal it, I have to put a note inside for your mother too, there's no point in sending two letters.'

Peggy slipped her letter into the envelope and began to pack the writing things away.

'Leave them out, please, Margaret. I have a couple of letters to write. I may as well do them at the same time as I write to Mrs Larkin.'

Peggy took a new candle from the cupboard, lit it with a match and held it over an old saucer to allow the hot wax to drip onto it, then she set the candle in the wax and said goodnight to Mrs Henderson.

Mrs Henderson raised her eyebrows. 'It's only eight o'clock, don't you want to listen to the radio for a while?'

Peggy yawned a jaw-cracking yawn. 'I'm not used to getting up quite so early, I'm really tired.'

'Would you like a nice hot bath before bed?'

Peggy's eyes lit up. 'Could I? I only get to have a bath on Sunday nights at home and I always have to go in after Harry.'

'Do you have a bathroom at home?' asked Mrs Henderson.

'No,' said Peggy. 'We have a big steel bath that Mum carries in from the scullery. It takes her ages to fill it up and empty it.'

Mrs Henderson led Peggy up the stairs to the first floor landing and opened a door on the left. 'I have a proper bathroom here, Margaret,' she said. 'You may bathe twice a week. I normally run a bath on Wednesday and Sunday, so you may as well do the same. Don't empty it when you get out. I'll go in after you to save money on heating the water. Don't stay in too long either; I don't like a cold bath.'

Mrs Henderson ran the bath until it was about one third full, then she dripped a few drops of lavender oil into it and checked the temperature by dipping her elbow in the water.

'My mum does that,' laughed Peggy.

'All mothers do it. You can't risk the water being too hot when you bathe your children.' Mrs Henderson's looked at her feet for a moment, then turned away and walked briskly from the room. 'Fifteen minutes, then it's my turn,' she said.

When Mrs Henderson came back up Peggy was out of the bath and was drying her hair in front of a steamy mirror dressed in her vest and pants. Mrs Henderson made a tutting noise when she saw how thin Peggy's underwear was.

'How many sets of vests and pants did you bring, Margaret?'

'I've got three sets, but these are the oldest, said Peggy. 'Mum was a bit worried about them when she packed my case.'

'I think I had better get you some new things when I go to town on Friday,' said Mrs Henderson. 'I have a committee meeting, so I'll nip into the shops and see what they have.'

Peggy looked worried. 'I don't think Mum can afford to buy me anything expensive.'

Mrs Henderson sat on a small stool at the side of the bath and took off her slippers. 'I won't be buying you anything expensive my girl, so don't worry about that. As it happens, now that you are billeted with me, I will receive ten shillings a week from the government. That will go some way towards the cost. Your mother won't have to pay a penny.'

Peggy left the bathroom and ran up the stairs to her room. She whispered goodnight to her mother and was asleep almost as soon as he head hit the pillow.

CHAPTER EIGHT

The following morning, Peggy woke as soon as Mrs Henderson opened her bedroom door.

'Rise and shine, Margaret Larkin. The sun's about to get up and so should you.'

'I'm already awake,' said Peggy. 'Are we doing anything today?'

'After breakfast I need you to go to Mr Brown's farm to pick up some fresh milk, then you have to lay the fire. I'll show you where the coal is and where to put the cinders when you come down.'

Peggy washed her face, cleaned her teeth and hurried downstairs to the kitchen. She was really keen to go to the farm. Mrs Henderson was amused.

'I've never seen anyone so eager to fetch milk,' she laughed.

'I've never been on a farm before. I can't wait to see all the animals,' said Peggy.

Peggy wolfed her breakfast down and quickly washed her bowl in the sink. 'How do I get to the farm?' she asked.

Mrs Henderson handed Peggy a large jug and gave her directions. 'Go out of the front door, turn right, walk for a quarter of a mile and you're there. It shouldn't take you more than half an hour to get there and back. You can see the farm from the first floor window.'

'I might be a little longer than that, because it's my first day,' said Peggy. 'Does Mr Brown have any chickens?'

Mrs Henderson frowned. 'Yes, he's a farmer. He has chickens, geese, cows, sheep, everything a farmer should have.'

Peggy began to get excited. She pulled on her shoes while she sat on the front doorstep and hurried out onto the narrow lane that ran along the side of Mrs Henderson's house.

Peggy followed the lane until it came to a five-barred gate with a piece of rope dropped over a post to keep it shut. She slipped the rope over the post, pushed the gate open and walked down the dirt track lane that led to the farm.

The track ended at a stone wall with an open gate in the centre. Beyond the gate was a muddy yard with a barn at one end and a large stone house at the other. Smoke rose from a tall chimney on the roof. Peggy walked towards the house but stopped dead as a black and white collie dog ran towards her, barking madly.

The dog stopped a couple of feet in front of Peggy. It pulled back its lips and snarled angrily. Peggy took a step back and her foot landed in something soft and warm. She looked down to see she had trodden in a cowpat.

'Oh yuck.'

'Taffy, come,' called a young voice.

The dog immediately turned and headed off towards the sound of the voice. Peggy's eyes followed it as it trotted across the farmyard towards the barn. In the doorway stood a boy of about Peggy's age. He wore a blue knitted jumper, a woollen cap, long grey shorts and Wellington boots that left just his knees exposed. His freckled face lit up in a smile as he walked out onto the farmyard.

'Careful where you walk,' said the boy. 'I haven't cleaned up all the cow muck yet.'

'Too late, I found some,' said Peggy lifting up her foot.

'I'm Alfie Garner, what's your name?'

'Peggy Larkin. I've been evacuated here.'

'Me too,' said the boy. 'I've been here a few days now, what are your new people like?'

'A bit strict,' said Peggy. 'I'm in the big house up the lane.'

'The Browns are a bit strict too,' said Alfie. 'They shaved my head the first night I got here.'

'I heard,' said Peggy. 'I was lucky, no nits.'

Alfie suddenly had a thought. 'Did you remember to shut the gate when you came in?'

'No, I don't think I did,' said Peggy. 'Does it matter?'

'It will if all the cattle get out,' replied Alfie. 'Come on, we'd better check.'

Alfie led Peggy back up the dirt track to the wooden gate. Half a dozen cows were on the other side of the gate chewing grass in the lane. Alfie picked up a long stick and tapped the cows on the backside until they moved back into the field, then he closed the gate and slipped the rope over the post to secure it.

'First rule of the countryside, never leave a gate open,' he said.

Peggy assured him and said she would be more careful next time and the pair walked back down to the farm. They were met in the yard by Mrs Brown.

'Are you skiving again, Alfie Garner?'

'No, Mrs Brown. I was just looking after Peggy here.'

'Peggy? Ah yes, you'll be the girl staying with Mrs Henderson. I hope you shut the gate behind you or we'll have cattle running amok in the village again.' She looked at Alfie through narrowed eyes.

'Yes, it's shut,' said Peggy.

'Well done. Not everyone remembers, do they Alfie?' Mrs Brown shot another glance at the young boy.

'No, Mrs Brown, it wasn't my fault though, there were too many things to remember...'

Mrs Brown shook her head and wagged a finger at the boy. 'I doubt if you can remember your name most days, Alfie Garner. You were given one simple instruction, and you forgot to remember it. Now then, is that barn mucked out? I'll be over to check soon.'

Alfie winked at Peggy and ran back to the barn. Mrs Brown turned her attention to Peggy. 'Come for milk have you? Give me the jug and I'll fill it for you.'

The farmer's wife disappeared through a door at the side of the house. When she returned she handed Peggy a full jug and a damp rag.

'Here, girl, clean your shoes before you go back home. Mrs Henderson won't want cow muck over her nice clean floors.'

Peggy gave her shoe a wipe down and passed the dirty cloth back to Mrs Brown. The farmer's wife dropped it into a bin and turned back to Peggy. 'Don't forget to shut the gate behind you, Peggy Larkin.' She looked towards the barn and laughed. 'We had to herd up the cattle from the village the morning after Alfie arrived. He wasn't the most popular boy in the neighbourhood that day I can tell you.'

Peggy almost told her about making the same mistake but decided against it.

'I'll have a word with Alfie next time I see him,' she said to herself as she walked out of the farmyard. 'First rule of the countryside indeed.'

Peggy carried the milk jug carefully back to the gate and placed it gently on the grass while she slipped the rope over the post. As she pulled the gate open she heard a twig snap. She looked round to see the figure of a man hurrying through the trees. Just before he disappeared from view he looked back over his shoulder. Peggy would know those eyes anywhere.

It was the man she had seen from the back of the cart.

CHAPTER NINE

Peggy rushed back to Mrs Henderson's house as fast as she could, every few seconds she looked over her shoulder to make sure she wasn't being followed. By the time she reached the house she had splashes of milk down the front of her jumper. Peggy ran up the steps, threw open the door and rushed into the kitchen.

'I've just seen...'

'Shoes!'

'But I've...'

'Margaret Larkin, I'm sure what you have to say is very important to you, but a clean floor is very important to me, you know the house rules,' said Mrs Henderson sharply.

Peggy banged the jug down onto the table and ran back to take off her shoes. When she returned to the kitchen Mrs Henderson was putting the jug on the cold shelf.

'It's barely half full, have you been drinking it on the way home?'

'No, I spilt some when I was running,' said Peggy.

Mrs Henderson looked puzzled. 'Why were you running with a jug full of milk?'

'I saw that man again...the one in the woods,' said Peggy.

Mrs Henderson frowned. 'Did you indeed. Where was this man?'

'Hiding in the bushes just this side of the farm gate, he saw me and took off. He's up to no good, I'm sure of it,' said Peggy.

Mrs Henderson tutted. 'I'm sure there's a simple explanation, Margaret, it may be a villager setting a rabbit trap or something, it happens all the time around here.'

'He ran when he realised I'd seen him though,' said Peggy. 'If he had nothing to hide he wouldn't do that.'

'He might if he was embarrassed at being caught,' replied Mrs Henderson. 'I'm sure there is an innocent explanation. I tell you what, why don't you have a word with PC Watson when he does his rounds, he comes by here most days.'

'I will,' said Peggy, 'There's something very odd about him.'

Mrs Henderson led Peggy through to the sitting room to show her how she wanted the fire laid in the mornings. The fire had burned out overnight and there was nothing but ashes in the grate. At the side of the fire was a pair of steel tongs, a poker and a brass coal scuttle.

'I do the fire at home sometimes,' said Peggy proudly. 'Dad says my fires light better than his even.'

Mrs Henderson showed Peggy where the ash bucket and dustpan were kept, then took her round the back of the house to show her where to empty it after she had cleaned the grate.

'I'll show you where the coal is kept next, follow me.'

Peggy followed Mrs Henderson to the front of the house. Under the bay window was a trapdoor that lay flat to the ground. Mrs Henderson took hold of the iron handle and, with a grunt, lifted it open.

'It's fairly heavy so you'll have to be careful.'

Peggy looked down into the dark coal cellar.

'This is where we keep the coal,' said Mrs Henderson. 'The coalman brings us five bags every two weeks, so we have to be careful with it, especially in the winter.'

Peggy nodded. 'Dad has to find bits of scrap wood when we run out of coal at home.'

If you're careful with the coal, we won't have to go searching for wood, Margaret,' said Mrs Henderson. 'Now listen carefully, this is important.' Mrs Henderson waited until she was sure she had Peggy's full attention before she continued.

'The coalman parks his horse and cart on the lane, carries the bags here and tips them into the cellar, then he drops the door shut. If ever you see it open, drop it immediately, I don't want to fall into the cellar on a dark winter's night. He has forgotten to shut it on more than one occasion.'

'How do I get the coal out? asked Peggy. 'There isn't a ladder.'

Mrs Henderson closed the trapdoor and made the tutting sound again. 'Follow me.'

She led Peggy back into the hall, opened a door next to the sitting room and pointed to a small shelf on the wall where a candle and a box of matches sat.

'That's for winter when it's still dark outside. On light mornings you'll be better off opening the hatch so the light gets in. Don't forget to close it again after you have filled the coal scuttle.'

Mrs Henderson pointed to a pair of old flat shoes that lay on the floor. 'Slip those on, light the candle and fill the scuttle. Remember to take them off when you reach the top of the stairs again; I don't want coal dust all over my nice clean floor.'

Peggy slipped her feet into the shoes, struck a match and lit the candle. The flame cast strange shadows on the walls. Mrs Henderson nudged her in the back and told her to get on with it. 'There aren't any ghosts down there, you might find the odd mouse but that's about it.'

Peggy wished Mrs Henderson hadn't mentioned ghosts. She took each step very slowly until she reached the bottom. The cellar was damp and musty with old cobwebs hanging from the walls. In the corner of the room was a dusty table, two chairs and wooden stepladder.

'Hurry up, we haven't got all day,' urged Mrs Henderson.

Peggy walked briskly to the coal pile and filled the coal scuttle to the brim. She tried to ignore the voice in her head that told her to look into dark shadows in the corner. *There were no ghosts, Mrs Henderson had said so.*

Peggy retraced her steps, climbed the stairs and stepped out of the shoes. She put the coal scuttle down, licked her fingers and put out the candle. Then she picked up the scuttle again and carried it through to the sitting room. Mrs Henderson was waiting for her.

'There, that wasn't so bad was it?'

Peggy wanted to say that it was very bad indeed and that she didn't like the cellar at all, but she remained silent. She had already made up her mind that she would open the cellar trapdoor every morning before she went to get the coal, whether it was dark outside or not.

*****

Peggy gave Mrs Henderson a hand with the washing and carried piles of clothes to and from the airing cupboard on the first floor while Mrs Henderson started on the ironing. After the second trip Peggy became intrigued by the door on the left hand side of the corridor.

What was in there that had to be kept so secret? Maybe Mrs Henderson kept her valuables in there, maybe there was a chest full of gold, or a map that led to buried treasure?

Peggy told herself to ignore all the questions and do as she had been told, but her mind nagged away, telling her that there was a secret to be discovered. Peggy found herself tiptoeing towards the door and before she knew it she was turning the handle.

'Margaret Larkin, get away from there this instant. That door is locked and out of bounds.'

Peggy stepped away as the tall figure of Mrs Henderson bore down on her.

'Sorry, Mrs Henderson, I was just...'

'I can see what you were just about to do, girl. You were going to do what I had explicitly told you not to do.'

Peggy looked at her feet. 'Sorry, it won't happen again, I...'

'You are correct, it won't happen again, young lady,' said Mrs Henderson, sternly. 'If it does you'll be for the high jump, do I make myself clear?'

Peggy nodded and studied her feet again.

'We'll forget about it this time, but there are no more chances, Margaret.' Mrs Henderson turned and walked back down the stairs. 'It's lunchtime,' she called over her shoulder. 'I'll warm up some broth. Hurry now.'

Over lunch Peggy studied the photograph of a young man in army uniform that stood on the sideboard. 'Who's that?' she asked.

'That is my husband, Frank,' said Mrs Henderson, proudly.

'He's very handsome,' said Peggy. 'I like his moustache, is he fighting in the war like my dad?'

'No, dear,' said Mrs Henderson. 'He fought in the First World War and lived to tell the tale. He also survived Spanish Flu in 1918 when millions died. We thought we would be together until we were old and grey, but he fell off a horse in 1927 and died. He was only thirty-seven.'

Mrs Henderson looked at the photograph and smiled sadly. Peggy felt so sorry for her. She began to wonder what it must be like to lose someone. *What if something happened to dad in the war?* She felt a tear in her eye and brushed it away with the back of her hand.

'Now, now, Margaret, there are no need for tears, things like this happen to people all the time. I miss him still, but we just have to get on with things.'

Peggy got up from her seat, walked round the table and gave Mrs Henderson a hug. Mrs Henderson smiled softly and gave Peggy a squeeze.

'This is something else I miss,' she said.

CHAPTER TEN

After lunch Mrs Henderson led Peggy to the study and told her to choose a book from the bookcase on the wall.

'I'm reading *The Hound of the Baskervilles* again,' she said. 'Sherlock Holmes is my favourite character, he's so clever at solving mysteries. I bet he'd find out the identity of your mystery man in no time.'

Surprisingly, there were several children's adventure books in the collection. Peggy chose *Winnie the Pooh,* and *The House at Pooh Corner* and carried them out to the kitchen. Mrs Henderson followed looking as though her mind was elsewhere.

Peggy had just opened the book and read the first line when there was a knock at the door.

'Answer that, Margaret, please.'

Peggy opened the door to find a policeman on the front step. He gazed down at Peggy with a surprised look on his face. 'Are you new?' he asked.

'Yes,' said Peggy. 'I'm Peggy Larkin, I'm staying with Mrs Henderson until the bombing stops.'

'Ah, you'll be the girl she rang me about. She couldn't find anyone else to take you then?'

Peggy remembered Sam Fettle and shuddered.

'Is Mrs Henderson in?' asked the policeman. 'I'd like a word if that's possible.'

Peggy opened the door and stood aside but the policeman stayed where he was.

'I don't really have time to take my boots off this afternoon,' he said. 'If you could just get her for me?'

'Ooh,' said Peggy. 'Before I do, can I report a suspicious person?'

The policeman took his notepad from his pocket, licked his pencil and waited for Peggy to give him the details. Peggy told him about the man she had seen hiding in the bushes.

'I've seen him twice now and both times he ran away when he realised I'd spotted him.'

The policeman put his pad back in his pocket and sighed. 'I need a bit more to go on than that, young lady. No one else has reported anything suspicious, I think it's just your imagination, you're putting two and two together to make five.'

'He's up to no good, I know it,' said Peggy. 'I bet you have to arrest him soon, he could be a German spy.'

The constable ignored her statement and looked over Peggy's head into the house. 'You were about to fetch Mrs Henderson to the door?'

Peggy walked back to the kitchen and told Mrs Henderson that the policeman wanted to see her. Mrs Henderson blushed and hurried to the wall mirror. She tidied her hair, smoothed down her dress, then turned to Peggy.

'Do I look all right?' she asked.

'You look all right to me,' said Peggy, wondering what the fuss was all about.

Mrs Henderson told Peggy to get back to her book, took a deep breath and left the room closing the door behind her. Peggy went back to the table and started the book again. She was half way through chapter two before Mrs Henderson came back. She appeared to be in a very good mood.

'How's the book?'

'Funny,' said Peggy. 'Winnie the Pooh has eaten too much honey and he's stuck in Rabbit's front door.'

'I love that story,' said Mrs Henderson, 'I used to read it to...' She tailed off and busied herself at the sink.

A few minutes later she put a saucepan full of water on the hob and began to chop vegetables.

'I'm going to leave you in charge on Friday afternoon when I go into town. PC Watson has business there too, so we're going to go in together. Will you be all right on your own?'

'I'll be fine,' said Peggy. 'I'll just sit and read.'

*****

The following morning Peggy opened the trapdoor to let light into the cellar, then rushed down the steps to fill the coal scuttle. She emptied the grate, laid the new fire then went back round to the front of the house to close the trapdoor. As she turned to go back in she heard a voice from the lane.

'Hello, Peggy.'

Peggy turned to find Alfie and Taffy at the gate.

'Bet it's dark down that cellar,' he said.

'Peggy nodded. 'I'm sure there's something horrible lurking down there.'

'There might be,' said Alfie. 'Ghosts like to lurk in cellars.'

'Don't,' said Peggy with a shudder. 'I try not to think about it.'

Alfie changed the subject. 'Are you coming for milk today?' he asked.

'Yes,' replied Peggy. 'I was just about to get the jug.'

Alfie crouched down and made a fuss of Taffy. 'I'll hang on then and walk with you.'

Peggy ran back inside and picked up the jug from the draining board. She called to Mrs Henderson as she ran back outside. 'Off for milk, back soon.'

Alfie sent Taffy off to search the hedgerows, then he picked up a stick and began a mock swordfight with an imaginary foe. Peggy walked behind smiling to herself.

'She's a nosey one isn't she?' said Alfie, suddenly.

'Who?' asked Peggy.

'The woman you're staying with, Anderson is it?'

'Henderson,' corrected Peggy.

'She was watching us as we walked away from the house,' said Alfie. 'I saw her at the upstairs window.'

'She's just keeping an eye on me I expect.' replied Peggy. 'There's a strange man in the woods, I've seen him twice now. He disappears when he knows I've spotted him.'

Alfie stopped fighting his invisible enemy and looked at Peggy with interest. 'A strange man? What does he look like? I'll keep my eye out for him.'

Peggy pulled a face. 'He's got a scruffy, torn coat on, he's got a beard and really horrible, narrow eyes.'

Alfie thought for a moment. 'Do you think he could be a German spy? I bet there're lots of them about.'

'He might be,' agreed Peggy.' He certainly doesn't want to be seen. I told PC Watson about him but he didn't really want to know. He thinks I'm imagining things.'

'If he's a German spy we could catch him, then we'd be famous,' said Alfie.

'I don't want to catch him, even if he is a spy,' said Peggy.

They reached the gate and Alfie opened it to allow Peggy to go through, then he carefully put the rope around the post. Peggy grinned to herself, she was tempted to ask if he'd ever forgotten to close it, but she decided against it.

At the farm, Alfie said goodbye and returned to his chores. Mrs Brown filled the jug and walked Peggy across the farmyard.

'See you next time, Peggy.'

Peggy looked up at the tree-lined lane and hesitated.

'What's the matter?' said Mrs Brown. 'Don't you fancy the walk?'

Peggy told Mrs Brown about the stranger in the bushes. The farmer's wife looked horrified.

'A stranger's in the woods? We can't have that... Alfie, get yourself over here you lazy pup.'

Alfie ran out of the barn with Taffy close on his heels.

'I want you to walk young Peggy home, Alfie, said Mrs Brown. 'If there is a stranger in the woods he won't bother two of you and you will be safe coming back with Taffy. Don't dawdle, that barn won't clean itself.'

Alfie and Peggy chatted about the different areas of London they lived in as they walked back. When they reached Mrs Henderson's house Alfie took a quick look at the upstairs window.

'She's there again, spying on you.'

Peggy laughed. 'She's probably just making sure I got back safely, that's all.'

Peggy thanked Alfie for walking her home and started up the path to the house. As she reached the door, Alfie called to her.

'Do you fancy coming out this afternoon? I'll show you the den I've built down by the river.'

Peggy grinned. 'I'll have to ask Mrs Henderson, but it should be all right.'

'Good,' said Alfie. 'I'll call for you at one.'

*****

By the time Peggy had removed her shoes Mrs Henderson was back in the kitchen. Peggy placed the milk jug on the cold shelf and sat down for breakfast.

'Mr Brown told Alfie to walk me home in case that man was around,' Peggy explained.

'I wondered who you were talking to. He's the boy who had to have his head shaved isn't he?'

Peggy nodded. 'Yes, that's Alfie. He wants me to go out this afternoon if that's all right with you?'

Mrs Henderson thought for a moment. 'I suppose so, where are you going?'

'Down to the river I think. Alfie's built a den.'

'Well, be careful,' said Mrs Henderson. 'I don't want to have to write to your mother to tell her you've had to be rescued from the river. Now, eat up your porridge before it gets cold.'

*****

When Peggy had washed her plate in the sink and put it on the drainer to dry Mrs Henderson went through to the sitting room and turned on the radio to listen to the news. Peggy sat with her for a few minutes but was soon lost in the jumble of announcements and reports. She had no idea where her father was, or even if he had left the country yet. She crossed her fingers and wished him good luck, wherever he was.

Mrs Henderson got out her sewing box and went upstairs to get a jumper that needed darning. Peggy picked up *Winnie the Pooh* and sat down in a comfortable high-backed chair to read. As she turned to her bookmarked page she heard a scraping sound from outside. Peggy left her book on the chair and looked out of the window.

Outside, a soft autumn breeze blew through the Sycamore leaves and the last of the summer flowers danced in the borders around the lawn. Peggy stood on her tiptoes and craned her neck to get a better look. She had just decided that she must have imagined the noise when a man's grimy face appeared at the window.

CHAPTER ELEVEN

Peggy screamed and ran from the room. Mrs Henderson rushed down the stairs to see what all the fuss was about.
'There's a face, a man, at the window.'

Mrs Henderson picked up a thick walking stick from the hall and rushed to the front door. She flung it open and leapt out onto the steps with a yell. Finding no one there she stormed round the side of the building holding the stick above her head. When she reached the front of the house she was greeted by the coalman.

'Hello, Mrs Henderson, hope I didn't scare the young 'un just then. I was just checking to see if you were in.'

Mrs Henderson leant on the walking stick and laughed to herself. 'You did give her a bit of a fright, Bert. Come round to the door and I'll get my purse to pay you.'

*****

Peggy felt stupid. *Why had she screamed like that? She wasn't a little girl any more, she was ten now.* Mrs Henderson took it all in good grace and put a hand on Peggy's shoulder as they walked to the kitchen.

'Better safe than sorry, Margaret. He isn't actually due until Monday so even I was surprised to see him.'

Peggy felt a little better after that. Mrs Henderson put the kettle on and made a nice cup of tea to settle their nerves.

*****

After lunch Peggy waited in the lane for Alfie to arrive, he got there ten minutes late and apologised immediately.

'Sorry I'm late, someone left the gate open again. I had to find three missing cows.'

'It wasn't me this time,' said Peggy.

'I know,' laughed Alfie. 'It could have been our German spy. Mrs Brown says she saw a stranger hanging around in the fields early this morning.'

'Get her to tell PC Watson. He wouldn't believe me,' said Peggy.

'She said it's probably just a tramp looking for somewhere dry to sleep.' replied Alfie.

'He's no tramp,' said Peggy. 'He's up to no good.'

Alfie led her down the lane for a hundred yards then turned into the woods. They followed a narrow path between the trees until they came to a shallow stream. Alfie took off his boots and stepped into the water.

'Come on, cross here, it gets a bit deeper further on.'

Peggy took off her shoes and socks and stepped into the stream, the water was icy cold. 'Brrr, it's freezing,' she complained.

Peggy ran across the stream as fast as she could. She was sure her feet would turn to ice if she remained in the water too long. As she sat down on the bank to pull on her socks, Alfie passed her some large dock leaves.

'Dry your feet with those or you'll have wet socks.'

Peggy thanked him and rubbed at her feet to try to get some warmth back into them.

'Anyone would think you were country born and bred, Alfie.'

'I learn quickly, you have to where I live. It's not the friendliest of places.'

'It's pretty friendly in our part of London,' said Peggy. 'The houses aren't as nice as they are out here but most people get on with each other.'

'Some people would steal from their own grandmothers where I live,' said Alfie.

'That's a shame. Maybe you're better off here then.'

'I am,' said Alfie. 'I get fed three times a day here. At home I'm lucky if we have one meal a day. I'm hoping if I work hard they'll let me stay, even after the bombing finishes. It's no fun being hungry all the time.'

Peggy had never been hungry in her life, not really hungry. 'I always get two meals and sandwiches for lunch at home,' she said. 'I know that a lot of my friends only get one meal though. Katie Withers used to share my lunch at school because she never got any breakfast.'

They followed the stream through the trees until it ran into a wider body of water. Alfie led Peggy along the left hand bank until they came to a plank bridge.

'Be careful here, some of the planks are missing,' he advised.

Peggy walked carefully over the bridge. There were quite a few planks missing but she easily stepped over the gaps and in no time at all she stood on the opposite bank feeling quite proud of herself.

'It's just along here,' whispered Alfie.

He led Peggy along the riverbank until they came to an old willow. The tree was bent over the river as if taking a drink. Beneath its branches a paddling of ducks made their leisurely way downstream. Peggy was fascinated by the ducks, she had never seen one close up before. When she looked back to the path, Alfie had disappeared.

Peggy ducked underneath the branches of the willow and wandered down the path for a few yards before returning to the spot where the ducks were swimming; there was no sign of Alfie. Peggy was just about to shout his name when there was a rustling of leaves and Alfie appeared on the path grinning from ear to ear.

'This way.'

Alfie lifted a door made from twigs and leaves and led her into the den. Inside he had made a waterproof roof from a tarpaulin sheet, the floor was covered with a tatty carpet and along one wall was an old case with three dirty cushions on top. Peggy looked around with her mouth open, Alfie looked on proudly.

'You can't see it at all from outside, even right up close, you are clever,' said Peggy.

'It only took me two afternoons to build, said Alfie. 'The hardest bit was dragging the tarp from the farm.'

'I bet no one would find you here if you needed to hide,' said Peggy.

Alfie grinned and pointed to tiny hole in the door. 'I built a spy hole so I can see if anyone comes sneaking up.'

Alfie lifted the lid of the case and pulled out a bottle of warm lemonade. He pulled out the stopper, wiped the neck of the bottle on his sleeve and offered it to Peggy before drinking some himself.

'I don't know how well it will stand up to the winter, but we'll find out soon enough. I want to sleep out here so I can listen to the sounds of the woods at night.'

'I don't think Mrs Henderson would let me stay out all night,' said Peggy, sadly.

'You never know, she might decide to stay with friends and leave you alone one night.'

Peggy brightened as she had an idea. 'Are you free tomorrow afternoon?'

Alfie nodded. 'I think so. Until school starts up I have to work in the mornings, but I get time to myself in the afternoons. Why do you ask?'

Peggy took another look through the spy hole, then turned back to face Alfie. 'Mrs Henderson is going into town tomorrow afternoon and I'm going to be on my own, I'll ask her if you can come over if you like?'

'That would be great,' said Alfie.

He produced a homemade cane fishing rod and a small tin containing small lumps of bread from the case. Peggy wondered what else he had hidden away in there.

'Let's see if the ducks have left any fish in the river,' he said.

'I've never been fishing before,' said Peggy.

'I used to fish in the canal at home,' said Alfie. 'I caught a pike once, but that was with my uncle's fishing rod, this one isn't as good.'

Alfie lifted the twig door and propped it open with a forked stick, then he bought out two of the cushions and they sat on the edge of the river where they swopped stories, told silly jokes and took it in turns to fish. They caught nothing all afternoon. Alfie said it was because the bread was stale.

Mrs Henderson was waiting for Peggy as she and Alfie walked slowly up the lane towards the house. Peggy thought she was going to be angry but she just smiled and asked if they had had a nice time.

'Yes thanks, Mrs Henderson. We've had great fun.'

She began to explain about the den but a dig in the ribs from Alfie stopped her. Instead she asked if it would be all right for Alfie to come over the next day.

'I don't see why not,' she replied. 'The Browns are reasonably happy with him, so I suppose I can trust him with the family silver.'

'Come over at half past one,' said Peggy. She turned to Mrs Henderson. 'Can I make us sandwiches for lunch tomorrow?'

Mrs Henderson made her familiar tutting noise and shook her head. 'I'll make the sandwiches, young lady, I don't think my last pot of shrimp paste would go very far in your hands.'

Alfie said goodbye and headed back to the farm while Peggy and Mrs Henderson went in to make tea. Later they listened to the Ovaltinies show on the radio before Peggy fell asleep in the chair. Mrs Henderson woke her at eight to tell her if she slept much longer she would find it hard to sleep when she went to bed, but at nine o'clock Peggy put her head on the pillow and didn't stir until morning.

CHAPTER TWELVE

Alfie knocked on the door at one thirty on the dot. Mrs Henderson let him in and watched him take off his shoes before leading him through to the kitchen. Peggy sat at the table writing a letter home.

'Hello, Peggy.'

Mrs Henderson tutted. 'I think you'll find her name is Margaret, or at least it is when she's in this house.'

Alfie winked at Peggy and sat down opposite her at the table. Mrs Henderson looked in the mirror, patted her hair, then walked to the sink before checking herself in the mirror again. A few minutes later PC Watson knocked on the door. Mrs Henderson checked the mirror again before giving Peggy her final instructions.

'Behave yourselves now, don't go making a mess and if you go out, pull the catch down on the door. You'll find a key to the back door under the upturned plant pot next to the greenhouse.'

She checked the mirror again then walked to the door. 'Sandwiches are on the plate under the tea towel. Make yourself tea if you want to, but go easy on the milk.'

Peggy nodded and raised her hand to wave. 'We'll be good, don't worry.'

Mrs Henderson checked the mirror one last time before hurrying out of the door.

'She's a vain one isn't she?' said Alfie. 'She'll wear that mirror out if she isn't careful.'

'I think she just wants to look nice for PC Watson,' said Peggy.

'Ah, I see,' said Alfie. 'Aren't' they a little old to be going out together?'

'That's what I thought,' said Peggy. 'She's over forty you know?'

Alfie shook his head. 'I don't know what the world's coming to, old people acting like young 'uns, it must be the war.'

*****

They chatted for a while, then Peggy put the plate of fish paste sandwiches on the table and made a pot of tea. Peggy only ate two but Alfie ate as though it was to be his last meal. When the plate was empty he looked around to see if there was any more, then, seeing there wasn't, he pushed his chair back and put both hands on his stomach.

'That's better; I was so hungry I could have eaten a horse.'

Peggy laughed. 'Farmer Brown ought to keep his eye on his then. If it goes missing we all know who to blame.'

Peggy walked Alfie through to the sitting room and turned on the radio. A dance band was playing and they sang along to some of the hit songs of the day. After a while Alfie asked where the lavatory was and Peggy showed him upstairs.

'Wow! This is a big place isn't it?' he said. 'You could get lost in here.'

'My room's right at the top,' said Peggy. 'You can hear the house creaking at night from up there.'

'What's down here?' asked Alfie.

'Mrs Henderson's room and a couple of guest rooms but there's no furniture in them,' replied Peggy.

Alfie walked across the landing. 'What about along here?'

Peggy stayed where she was. 'I'm not allowed down there.'

'Why not?' asked Alfie.

'I'm just not,' said Peggy. 'It's a house rule. Come on, let's go back down.'

Alfie walked down the corridor and tried the handle of the door just beyond the bathroom.

'It's locked,' he said.

'I know,' replied Peggy. She took hold of Alfie's arm. 'Come on, let's...'

'Why is it locked, do you know?'

Peggy shook her head. 'No, she won't say, she just told me to keep out.'

'Don't you want to know what's in there? said Alfie. 'There might be a dead body or something.'

'There isn't. Mrs Henderson isn't likely to have killed anyone,' said Peggy.

Alfie wasn't convinced. 'She might have a mad sister locked away in there. I saw a film once, the...'

'She hasn't,' said Peggy.

Alfie studied the lock carefully. 'I reckon I could pick this lock.'

'Don't you dare...'

Alfie looked up at Peggy, then turned his attention to the lock again. 'It wouldn't take a minute. I could lock it again afterwards.'

Peggy remained silent.

'Shall I try?'

'Be quick then,' said Peggy. 'Straight in and out again.'

'Do you know where she keeps her sewing kit?' asked Alfie. 'I'll need a darning needle and a crochet hook.'

Peggy bought the sewing box upstairs. Alfie took a long look at the lock, then selected a needle and hook. He pushed the darning needle into the bottom of the keyhole then slid in the hook and wriggled it about. A few seconds later there was a click and Alfie turned the handle to open the door.

'I hope you can lock it as easily,' said Peggy. 'Where on earth did you learn to do that?'

Alfie winked. 'You learn lots of things when you have to.'

Peggy looked into the dark room. The heavy curtains were pulled shut, the air smelt musty.

Alfie stepped into the room, edged his way over to the window and yanked at the curtains to pull them open. The daylight burst into the room highlighting the clouds of dust that littered the air.

'It's been a while since anyone came in here,' he said.

Peggy walked through the door and looked around. The made-up bed was covered with dusty old teddy bears and dolls. At one end of the room sat a cobweb-covered, wooden rocking horse with a red painted saddle. The walls were covered in children's drawings. On the table by the bed was a dusty old saucer in which sat a half burned candle. On a chair nearby was a neatly folded nightgown, a soft towel hung over the back.

Peggy wrote her name in the dust on the table with her finger. 'This is so strange, the rest of the house is spotless.'

Peggy walked across to a dark wood wardrobe and pulled open the door. Inside were hangers full of young girls' clothes. She took out a party frock and held it up in front of her.

'This is nice, I could...'

'Put that back now! What on earth do you think you are doing?'

Peggy jumped at the sound of Mrs Henderson's voice.

Once he had recovered from the shock of being caught, Alfie tried to take the blame. 'It was my fault Mrs...I ...'

'Get out of my house,' shouted Mrs Henderson.

Alfie tried again. 'It wasn't Peggy's fault she...'

'I won't tell you again,' screamed Mrs Henderson. 'Get out before I call PC Watson.'

Alfie knew when he was beaten. He rushed to the door and hared down the stairs.

'Sorry, Peggy,' he called as he ran.

Angry tears poured down Mrs Henderson's face. She pointed to the door and hissed at Peggy. 'Get out of my sight before I say something I might regret.'

'I'm sorry, Mrs Hen...'

'OUT!'

Peggy walked slowly past Mrs Henderson and headed for her room. Mrs Henderson locked the door and stormed downstairs.

'Don't bother coming down for tea, Margaret Larkin, there won't be any. I should never have bought you here. I might just ring Sam Fettle and tell him to come and get you.'

Peggy closed her bedroom door and threw herself down on her bed, her body racked with sobs. She doubted there was anything she could do to make it up to Mrs Henderson. She had betrayed her trust and now she was in deep trouble. Saying sorry wasn't going to be enough this time.

Peggy lay on her back and stared at the ceiling, her mind in a whirl. Mrs Henderson was furious. *What if she was talking to Sam Fettle on the telephone to say he could come round and pick her up in the morning?* She couldn't allow that to happen. She packed her clothes into her case and placed it by the door, then she settled back on the bed and began to cry again.

'I'm coming home, Mum. If I can find the way,' she sobbed.

CHAPTER THIRTEEN

Peggy tried her hardest to stay awake until she was sure Mrs Henderson had gone to bed, but by nine o'clock she had fallen fast asleep. She woke at two, to the sound of someone crying.

Peggy slowly opened her door and crept down the stairs to the floor below. The crying and sniffling got louder as she descended. Peggy followed the sound and found Mrs Henderson sitting on the floor outside the locked room. Her knees were tucked under her chin, she rocked back and forth as she talked to herself.

'I'm sorry I wasn't a good mother, Katie. I tried my best but it just wasn't enough. Forgive me, please?'

Mrs Henderson cried for a while then began to talk again.

'I should have insisted that you go to hospital. It's all my fault. You should be here with me now, not some London girl who can't do as she is told.'

Mrs Henderson rocked back and forth until the tears became sniffles. Peggy turned and began to climb the stairs, but when Mrs Henderson began to cry again she decided she had to do something to comfort her.

Peggy walked slowly up to Mrs Henderson and crouched down at her side. The woman continued to rock back and forth. Peggy reached out a hand to touch her shoulder but pulled it back as her eyes flashed open.

'Who's there? Is that you, Katie?'

Mrs Henderson sat bolt upright and stared straight ahead. Peggy waved a hand in front of her eyes but she didn't even blink.

Peggy had heard stories of people walking around while they were still fast asleep. Grandma had told her about the time Granddad went the shops in the middle of the night dressed only in his pyjamas.

Peggy realised that Mrs Henderson was sleepwalking and it could be very dangerous, even inside the house. She could easily trip and fall down the stairs. Peggy decided to try to wake her up.

When Mrs Henderson had settled again, Peggy leant forward and whispered to her.

'Mrs Henderson, it's me, Peggy. Wake up Mrs Henderson, you should be in bed.'

Mrs Henderson didn't appear to hear, instead she began to cry again.

'Oh, Katie, what did I do wrong? If only I had another chance.'

Peggy leaned forward again and placed her hand softly on Mrs Henderson's shoulder. 'Mrs Henderson, wake up, it's me, Peggy.'

'Katie?' Mrs Henderson's face lit up in a smile. 'Is that you, Katie?'

'No, it's Peggy, you have to wake up.'

Mrs Henderson grabbed hold of Peggy and hugged her tightly. 'Katie? Oh Katie, you've come back.'

Mrs Henderson began to weep uncontrollably. Peggy tried to ease herself away but couldn't move an inch. Suddenly Mrs Henderson's eyes shot open. She stared at Peggy with a confused look.

'You're not my Katie.'

'No, I'm Peggy, that's what I was trying to...'

'Get away from me.'

Mrs Henderson pushed Peggy away and got to her feet. 'Haven't you caused enough trouble for one day? Why are you sneaking around the house at this time of night?'

Peggy tried to explain. 'But... You were asleep, you were sleepwalking. I was scared you might fall and...'

'Go to your room you wicked girl,' shouted Mrs Henderson.

Peggy began to climb the stairs. When she was half way up she heard Mrs Henderson mutter to herself as she made her way back to her room.

'Wicked girl, pretending to be Katie...'

Peggy closed the bedroom door behind her and sat on her bed to think. She couldn't get out of the house while Mrs Henderson was patrolling the lower floor. She would have to wait until she was sure that Mrs Henderson was safely back in her bedroom. Peggy opened the thick blackout curtain and leaned back against the wall, a few seconds later she was asleep.

Peggy woke again just as it was getting light. She took her suitcase and tiptoed down to the first floor. Mrs Henderson's bedroom door was closed and she could hear the faint sound of snoring from inside the room. Feeling more confident, Peggy crept downstairs and eased open the door to the lobby. As she was about to pull on her shoes she decided she had better leave Mrs Henderson a note apologising for all the distress she had caused her.

Peggy took a sheet of notepaper from the drawer and sat down at the table to write.

Dear Mrs Henderson.

I am so sorry for going into the room on the first floor. If I had known how much it would hurt you I would never have done it. I was just curious to know what was inside. Alfie wouldn't have picked the lock if I hadn't told him about it, so please don't blame him.

I know that I can't stay with you any longer, so I'm going to try to find my way back to London. I hope you can find it in your heart to forgive me, I am truly sorry.

Love

Peggy xxx

Peggy folded the paper in half and placed it in the centre of the kitchen table so that Mrs Henderson would find it when she came down. She thought about taking some bread and cheese from the larder but decided against it. She didn't want to be labelled a thief as well as a troublemaker.

Peggy returned to the lobby and pulled on her shoes. As she fastened the straps she thought about the journey she was about to make. She had no idea which direction to take and because of the war all the signposts had been taken down.

'I'll ask Alfie, he might know which way to go,' she said to herself.

Peggy picked up her little case and stepped out of the front door. She was frightened by the prospect of having to find her own way back home, but there wasn't really any choice. The thought of spending the rest of the war slaving for Sam Fettle was even worse than the thought of getting lost in the wide open spaces of the countryside. Peggy wiped away a tear and told herself to be brave, but it didn't work. A few seconds later the tears were streaming down her cheeks.

Peggy took a deep breath, wiped her face on her sleeve and set off down the lane towards Brown's farm.

CHAPTER FOURTEEN

Peggy left her case by the wall at the edge of the farm and walked into the farmyard. Mrs Brown came out from the dairy and called to her in a stern voice.

'You're still here then, have you come for milk?'

Peggy decided to make out everything was the same as usual. 'Yes, Mrs Brown.'

'Aren't you ashamed of yourself, going into a dead girl's room like that? Beryl was so upset when she telephoned me last night.'

Peggy was shocked. 'Dead girl! I didn't know, I still don't know. I only went in there to see what the secret was. Mrs Henderson didn't tell me someone had died in there.'

Mrs Brown's manner softened as she saw how upset Peggy was. 'It was her daughter, Katie's room. She died of Scarlet Fever about ten years ago. She would have been about your age.'

Peggy gasped and held her hand to her mouth. 'I'm so sorry. I wish I had known. I wouldn't have gone anywhere near that room.'

Mrs Brown wiped away a tear, then continued. 'Beryl nursed Katie herself, there was no room in the isolation wards at the hospital. She blames herself for Katie's death; she doesn't think she nursed her well enough.'

Peggy looked crestfallen. 'Poor Mrs Henderson, no wonder she was so upset.'

'You tell her we're all thinking of her when you get back,' said Mrs Brown.

'I will,' said Peggy. 'Is Alfie about?'

Mrs Brown pointed across the farmyard. 'He's in the barn, mucking out. He's got extra chores as a punishment for picking locks. Go over and see him while I fill the jug...or did you forget to bring one?'

Peggy held out her empty hands. 'Sorry, I'm not thinking straight this morning.'

'Not to worry,' said Mrs Brown. 'You can borrow one of ours, I'll leave it by the back door. Don't keep Alfie talking too long, he's got a long day ahead of him.'

*****

Peggy found Alfie spreading new straw onto the floor of the barn. Taffy wagged his tail at her as she approached.

'Hello, Peggy.' said Alfie. 'How are things up there? I'm in a bit of bother here.'

'Bad,' said Peggy. 'I'm running away, I'm going home to London.'

Alfie's jaw dropped. 'Running away? It can't be that bad can it? Give it a day or so, it will all blow over.'

Peggy's eyes filled with tears. 'She said she's going to send me to live with that awful Sam Fettle.'

Alfie tried to reassure her. 'She wouldn't do that, she's the one who saved you from him.'

Peggy wasn't so sure. 'She's really angry, so she probably would.'

'How are you going to get to London? Do you have train fair, bus fare?'

Peggy shook her head. 'No, I don't even have a map. I haven't thought about how I'm going to get there, I only know I have to go.'

Alfie thought about things for a moment, then came to a decision. 'Right then. If you're going, I'm going too, I'm much more to blame than you are. I can't let you go off on your own.'

'But you love it here, Alfie,' said Peggy. 'Your life is so much better. I only came to say goodbye, not to ask you to come with me.'

Alfie walked to the barn door and looked out over the farmyard. 'I'd miss this place I have to admit, but I feel responsible. Anyway, you're my friend, Peggy, I wouldn't be able to sleep at night worrying about you. I can always come back once we've got you home safely.'

Peggy relaxed a little. 'If you're sure, Alfie. I'd hate to think you had to give up your new life, just for me.'

'Friends should stick together, especially when they are in trouble,' said Alfie. 'Do you have any food for the journey?'

'No,' said Peggy. 'I've got no money, no food, just my clothes. I left my case by the farmyard wall. I didn't want Mrs Brown to see it.'

'I don't know about money, but I can get us plenty of food,' said Alfie. He sat on a hay bale and thought for a moment. 'We'll be better off travelling at night, if we go in the daytime someone will spot us.'

'We could hide in the den until it gets dark?' suggested Peggy.

'I've just worked out a plan,' said Alfie. 'You go up to the den and wait there. I'll carry on as normal this morning and when I've finished my chores I'll bring some food and we'll take it from there. I'm not sure what time it will be though, they've given me extra work.'

'That sounds good,' said Peggy.

'Wait here a minute,' said Alfie. 'I'll get you something to drink.'

Alfie walked briskly across the farmyard with Taffy in hot pursuit. A few minutes later he was back with a bottle of water, a lump of cheese and a thick slice of bread.

'It's the best I can do for now. I'll try to get something better this afternoon.'

Peggy took the food and water and hid it under her jumper. Alfie walked her back to the farmyard gate to pick up her case.

'Can you remember the way?' he asked.

'Yes, I think so,' said Peggy. 'I'll find it all right.'

Alfie leaned forward to kiss Peggy on the cheek, but quickly changed his mind and held out his hand instead. Peggy shook it gently.

'Good luck, Peggy. I'll see you later,' he said.

Peggy walked quickly away from the farm, her mind a jumble of thoughts. Every few yards she looked behind to make sure she wasn't being followed. When she reached the wooden gate she checked the woods on both sides of the lane in case the stranger was lurking. She closed the gate behind her and walked up the lane for a hundred yards before she slipped through a hole in the hedgerow and into the woods.

'So far so good,' she said to herself.

Peggy found the stream and slipped off her shoes and socks before crossing. On the other side she found some big dock leaves to dry her feet, then pulled her shoes and socks back on and climbed the slope. On the far side she followed a narrow path until she came to the plank bridge. Peggy hurried across making sure she stepped over the missing planks and made her way to the riverbank. Five minutes later she pulled up the twig door and stepped into the den. She put her case on the floor, arranged the cushions on the case-seat, then sat down and had breakfast.

Peggy dozed off once or twice during the morning, she was bored sat around doing nothing. She began to wish she had brought *Winnie the Pooh* to read. She passed the time doing mental arithmetic puzzles. When she tired of that she drew grids on the floor with a stick and played noughts and crosses. At one-thirty she heard the crackle of branches and a whispered voice.

'Peggy, it's me.'

Peggy looked through the spy hole and saw Alfie waiting on the path with two paper bags full of food.

'This lot should keep us going for a day or two,' he said.

'A week more like. How are we going to carry it all?' laughed Peggy.

Alfie grinned. 'I've got a small case too, and as I'll be coming back here afterwards, I won't need to put much in it.'

Peggy pointed to the old case on the floor. 'Isn't that yours?'

Alfie shook his head. 'No, that was one I found in the barn. Mines about the same size as yours, I'll bring it over later.'

Peggy was disappointed. 'Are you going back then? I thought you were going to stay with me this afternoon?'

Alfie looked at her apologetically. 'I have a couple of bits to finish off, Peggy. I don't want them to get suspicious. I'll come over this evening after tea. Meanwhile I'll sort out my stuff and find us a map. I'll get back as soon as I can, I promise.'

Alfie left at two. Peggy looked in the food bags and found some bread and ham wrapped in greaseproof paper. In the bottom of one bag was a bottle of homemade lemonade. Peggy had lunch and sat down to wait again. Mid-afternoon she heard the shuffling of feet on the path outside the den. Peggy was about to open the door but decided to check the spy hole first. She couldn't see anyone on the path, but she heard the sound of a voice.

'This will do, William Travers. Let's just rest our bones here against this willow tree for a while.'

Peggy looked out to see the stranger standing on the path just a little further along from the den. Peggy gasped and stepped back from the spy hole, a small twig snapped under her foot with a sharp crack.

Peggy held her breath as the man walk towards the sound. She summoned up all her courage and peeped through the spy hole. She just managed to keep in a scream as she saw his face only a few inches away. His narrow eyes darted back and forth, then he began to sniff.

'Ham, in the middle of a wood?'

William laughed and turned away. 'You're imagining things, William,' he said to himself. 'But tonight, with luck, you'll be tucking into eggs and bacon, maybe even a nice fat sausage.'

William licked his lips and leant back against the tree. Peggy finally breathed out and sat down on the case. A few minutes later she heard the sound of snoring.

CHAPTER FIFTEEN

Peggy sat on the case hardly daring to move for almost three hours. As the shadows lengthened outside on the path, William decided that it was time to move on.

'Come on then, William. It's time to see who's home.'

William got up, stretched and began to walk up the path. When he reached the den he stopped and sniffed again.

'You've got ham on the brain, William,' he chuckled to himself. 'We had better go and find you some.'

Peggy waited until the footsteps had died away before she got to her feet. She was thirsty but she hadn't dared to drink in case William had heard. Peggy picked up the bottle of lemonade and took a long drink. She tried to judge the time but had only the vaguest idea. She decided to work on her eight times table to pass the time, she had just got to *eight eights are sixty four*, for the ninth time, when she heard the sound of running feet.

'Peggy. It's me, open up.'

Peggy opened the door and Alfie burst into the den. Before he could speak, Peggy blurted out her news. 'William was here.'

Alfie was puzzled. 'Who's William?'

'The stranger.'

Alfie's eyes popped wide open. 'He was in here? How did...'

'Not in the den, silly,' said Peggy. 'He sat with his back to the willow talking to himself. He only went about ten minutes ago, I'm surprised you didn't see him in the woods.'

'I didn't see anyone, maybe he knows another path back to the road.' said Alfie.

'Well, wherever he's gone, he thinks he's going to get a nice dinner,' laughed Peggy. 'He could smell my ham sandwich and it made him hungry.'

Alfie propped up the door with his forked stick and led Peggy out onto the path. Peggy looked for Alfie's suitcase but he hadn't brought it with him.

'I've got news, lots of it,' he said.

'News?'

'Mrs Henderson came down to the farm this afternoon, she was really upset. She told Mrs Brown that you had run away and showed her your letter. She was crying and kept saying, 'it's all my fault, that poor girl.'

'Poor Mrs Henderson,' said Peggy, sadly.

'She wanted to form a search party to find you, she really wants you to go back, Peggy.'

'She might just be feeling a little bit guilty,' said Peggy thoughtfully. 'She could still hand me over to Sam Fettle.'

'I don't think she will, Peggy, she seemed very concerned about you.'

Peggy sighed. 'I don't know, Alfie, she was very angry last night. I can't see her changing her mind that quickly.'

'I'm not so sure,' said Alfie.

Peggy sat down heavily on the big case and cupped her chin in her hands. 'You said you had lots of news?'

'Oh yeah, I do,' said Alfie. 'That's something else she's worried about. It seems that hundreds of evacuees have got Scarlet Fever. They must have brought it with them from London. All the hospitals have set up isolations wards. Mrs Henderson says they've been filling up since the trains began to arrive.'

'That's what her daughter died of isn't it?' said Peggy.

Alfie nodded. 'I think so, yes. She's worried that you have it and you're lying sick and alone somewhere.'

'I feel fine,' said Peggy. 'I don't think I have it.'

Alfie sat down on the case next to Peggy. 'The thing is,' he said. 'It can take a few days before you see any signs of it but some people get it the day after they come in contact with a carrier. I'm all right, I had it a few months ago. It spread like wildfire round our way. I was taken to hospital and put in quarantine.'

'Poor Mrs Henderson,' Peggy repeated.

'I think you should go and see her,' said Alfie. 'There may be no need to leave at all.'

Peggy thought for a while but rejected the idea. 'You didn't see her in the night when she was talking to herself. She hates me, she said I was wicked. I was only trying to comfort her.'

'Tell you what,' said Alfie. 'Why don't I go and see her for you? I can usually tell if someone is trying it on. You have to know when someone's trying to trick you where I come from.'

Peggy was delighted with the idea. 'Would you, Alfie? That would be great. If she really wants me to come back to stay, I will, but if she just wants to send me to someone else, then I'll go back to London.'

'Did you know she's got diabetes?' asked Alfie.

Peggy shook her head.

'Well, she has. She has to inject her medicine twice a day or she could die. I overheard her talking about it to Mrs Brown this afternoon. Mrs Brown wanted her to stay for tea but she said she had to get back to get her injection.'

'Poor Mrs Henderson,' said Peggy, again.

Alfie got to his feet and brushed the bits of leaf and twig from the seat of his shorts. 'I'll go and see her now, Peggy. With a bit of luck you could be back there in time for supper.'

'Shall I wait here or in the lane?' asked Peggy.

Alfie thought for a moment. 'Better wait here. If that William bloke is hanging around it's best not take any chances.'

Alfie ran off along the river bank while Peggy closed the twig door again and sat down to wait.

*****

Two hours later Peggy was seriously worried. *What had happened to Alfie? He should have been back a long time ago.* Peggy decided to walk down to the farm to see if the Browns had caught him and made him go home.

Peggy got to the farm just as the sun was setting. She hid behind the low wall at the edge of the farmyard and peeped over the top. Mrs Brown was in the yard with her husband. They were discussing Alfie.

'Where is that boy?' said Mrs Brown. 'He's been gone for almost three hours.'

'He'll be up in the woods in that den of his,' said Mr Brown.

'He's usually back by now, Henry. I'm getting a bit worried.'

Mr Brown patted his wife's hand. 'Give him another hour, if he's not back by then I'll get Taffy and go to look for him.'

Peggy crept away from the wall; she was seriously worried about Alfie. She wondered if he had bumped into William on his way to Mrs Henderson's house. Something had happened to him, that was for certain.

Peggy made her way back to the tied gate as the full moon began to rise. She felt very exposed as she walked along the lane towards Mrs Henderson's. She was tempted to walk in the shadow of the hedgerow but was worried about William grabbing her in the dark.

Peggy slowed as she neared the house. All seemed quiet. She walked up to the front door and was about to knock when she thought better of it. *'If Alfie had been talking to Mrs Henderson all this time then things can't have been going too well,'* she thought. Peggy decided to see if she could peek into the kitchen to see what was happening.

Peggy crept round to the kitchen window. The blackout curtain had been pulled shut but there was a crack of bright yellow light coming from one corner of the window.

'That's odd,' thought Peggy. Mrs Henderson only used candles and paraffin lamps to light the place. The light coming from the crack was much brighter than that.

Peggy tiptoed round the front door again and looked through the letterbox. She could see straight into the hall through the glass panel on the lobby door. The electric lights were on in the hallway too.

'There's something very wrong here,' muttered Peggy.

Peggy knew that Mrs Henderson would never leave all the lights on, even if she had decided to use the electricity again. She was about to close the letterbox when the figure of a large man moved across the hallway and stood at the bottom of the stairs. She heard the muffled sound of shouting followed by a short burst of laughter. As he turned to go back to the kitchen Peggy got a good look at his face. She gasped in horror. She would know those cruel eyes anywhere.

Peggy closed the letterbox quietly and stepped back from the door. 'What on earth is William Travers doing here?' she whispered to herself. 'And where is Mrs Henderson and Alfie?'

CHAPTER SIXTEEN

Peggy crept back to the laurel bushes in the front garden and thought about what to do next. *Why had William Travers shouted up the stairs like that? Maybe that's where Mrs Henderson was? Alfie might be in there too.* She thought about going to get PC Watson but if it turned out that Mrs Henderson had invited William Travers into the house, she might get into trouble for wasting the policeman's time. Peggy decided that she had to get inside to find out what was happening

'Think hard, Peggy. You need a plan,' she whispered to herself.

Peggy walked to the back of the house and tried the rear door. It was locked and the blackout curtain had been pulled across the glass. She checked the windows to see if any had been left open but they were all shut. Then she remembered the coal hole.

Peggy hurried round to the front and carefully pulled the trapdoor open. The moonlight shone into the cellar lighting up the large pile of coal that had been deposited yesterday.

Peggy stood at the edge of the coal hole and looked down into the shadows. Her knees shook as she thought about the dark creepy corner in the cellar. The hairs stood up on the back of her neck and she felt a shiver run down her spine.

'There's something in the corner,' said a voice at the back of her mind.

'There are no ghosts in the cellar, there are no ghosts in the cellar,' she told herself.

Peggy hesitated. Then she thought about Mrs Henderson and Alfie and the fear in her mind was replaced by a steely determination.

Peggy did the bravest thing she had ever done in her life. She closed her eyes and jumped into the darkness. She hit the coal pile with a thud and slid on her bottom to the concrete floor.

Peggy picked herself up, rubbed her backside and listened for any sign that she had been heard. Upstairs the radio was turned up high, Peggy could hear a dance band playing *Moonlight Serenade*. She looked up at the moon shining down into the cellar and thought it was the perfect song for the moment.

Peggy tried not to think about the dark corner and hurried up the steps to the cellar door. She eased it open a crack and looked out into the hall. From the kitchen she heard William Travers whistling along to the radio as he fried his bacon and eggs. Peggy eased the door open just wide enough for her to slide through, then closed it softly behind her. The door clicked as it closed. Peggy's head jerked round to see if he had heard but the sound of whistling continued. Peggy breathed a huge sigh of relief and tiptoed across the hall to the stairs.

The stairway was wide with a thick red carpet running up the centre. Peggy held onto the banister with one hand and climbed the stairs one slow step at a time, listening for the slightest creak that might alert William to her presence. When she reached the landing she crept along the corridor to Mrs Henderson's room. The door was open, so Peggy stepped inside.

Mrs Henderson had been tied to a chair with three pieces of clothesline. Her head leaned to one side and her eyes were closed. Peggy placed a hand on her shoulder and shook her gently. Mrs Henderson stirred but didn't wake up. Peggy tried again, harder this time, but she slept on.

Peggy walked round to the back of the chair and began to pick at one of the knots. She stopped as she heard a muffled sound coming from behind the open door. Peggy stepped quietly across the room and found Alfie tied to another chair. He was awake but he had a handkerchief stuffed in his mouth to act as a gag.

Peggy eased the gag from Alfie's mouth and went to the back of the chair to untie the rope around his wrists.

'Mrs Henderson isn't well,' he whispered.

'I can see that,' hissed Peggy as she worked at the knot.

Alfie was impatient. 'Hurry up, if he finds you here we're done for.'

Peggy tugged at the rope but Alfie was pulling the other way in a desperate attempt to free himself.

'Stop pulling and sit still,' whispered Peggy as loud as she dared. 'You're making the rope go tight as fast as I'm loosening it.'

Alfie sat still while Peggy undid the knot to free his hands, then he leant forward and untied the one holding his feet.

'We have to get to PC Watson, quickly,' he said. 'And Mrs Henderson needs the doctor, she's having a hypo.'

'A what-o?' said Peggy.

'A hypo, thingy,' repeated Alfie. 'I can't say the whole word, it's too complicated, but it means she needs something sweet to get sugar into her blood.'

Peggy tiptoed over to look at Mrs Henderson. 'How do you know?'

Alfie crept to the door and looked out onto the landing. 'She told me before she collapsed,' he said quietly. 'She told William too, but he just laughed and said, 'too bad.'

'She's unconscious, how are we supposed to get her to eat something sweet?' said Peggy.

Alfie shrugged and held out both hands. 'We need the doctor Peggy. We can't help her.'

Peggy moved behind Mrs Henderson's chair and began to untie her bonds. Alfie tapped her on the shoulder and shook his head.

'If William looks in he'll know someone's been here if she's untied. If we leave her as she is he might think everything is as he left it. He would have to look round the door to see if I was still there.'

Peggy hated to leave Mrs Henderson tied up, but she could see the reasoning.

'Right, let's go,' she whispered. 'We'll have to be very careful, Alfie, he's got every light in the house on.'

Peggy moved towards the door and listened for any sound from the hallway. She made a 'follow me' motion with her hand and crept to the top of the stair. She waited until Alfie had caught up before she looked around the corner of the balustrade to see if the stairs were clear.

Alfie tapped Peggy on the shoulder and leaned over to whisper in her ear. 'How did you get in?'

'Through the coal cellar,' she replied. 'I was thinking about leaving through the front door but he might have locked it and kept the key.'

Peggy motioned for Alfie to follow and began to creep down the stairs. She froze half way down as a shadow appeared on the floor of the hallway, but it vanished again as quickly as it had appeared.

At the bottom of the stairs Peggy stopped and waited for Alfie to catch up before she tiptoed across the hallway and eased the cellar door open. The radio blared out from the sitting room. Peggy wondered how he could bear to have it so loud. When Alfie had caught up, Peggy closed the door and walked slowly down the cellar steps. At the bottom she shushed Alfie and pointed to the open trapdoor above the pile of coal that lay shining like black diamonds in the moonlight.

'How do we get out?' asked Alfie. 'That coal pile isn't high enough.'

'Bother,' hissed Peggy. Then she remembered the stepladder in the corner. She pointed it out to Alfie. 'We'll use that.'

Alfie set the ladder up at the side of the coal pile and nodded to Peggy to go first. The ladder was just about the perfect height and Peggy only had to lean over a little to be able to pull herself out of the cellar. Peggy stepped back and waited for Alfie to climb out, then she pointed to the trapdoor and signalled for him to close it. Alfie nodded but as he grabbed the handle it slipped from his hand and the trapdoor closed with a resounding crash.

Alfie looked in horror as the blackout curtain was pulled back and the angry face of William Travers appeared at the window.

'RUN!' she shouted.

Peggy led the way as they ran for the cover of the woods on the far side of the lane. She leapt through a hole in the hedge and threw herself into the trees. When she looked back she saw Alfie slip as he tried to get through the gap. William yelled threats as he hurtled down the lane after them. Alfie regained his footing and dived into the woods after Peggy. They ran between the trees for fifty yards then Alfie pulled Peggy into a clump of thick bushes. They sat gasping for breath as William crashed through the woods back along the track. As he got closer they could hear him talking to himself.

'Quietly now, William, you'll find him... How did he manage to escape? You can't have tied him up tightly enough...We'll find him, he's around here somewhere. Maybe this stick will flush him out?'

William picked up a thick branch and began to poke it into the bushes at random.

'Come out, I know you're in here somewhere, it'll be worse for you if you don't give yourself up.'

Peggy and Alfie held their breath as he came closer. Suddenly the stick pierced the bush they were hiding behind. It missed Peggy by inches. She fought off the urge to scream and they sat hunched up and frightened until William moved further down the path. When he thought the man was out of earshot, Alfie tapped Peggy on the arm and leaned forward.

'He doesn't know you're here,' he whispered. 'He thinks it's just me.'

'How does that help us?' hissed Peggy.'

Alfie put his mouth close to Peggy's ear. 'If I were to jump out and run back the way we came, he'd follow me and you could run down to get PC Watson and the doctor.'

Peggy shook her head. 'You can't, Alfie, it's too dangerous.'

'It's the only way, Peggy. Anyway, it's embarrassing being rescued by a girl. I have to rescue you now so we can call it quits.'

Peggy let out a nervous giggle. 'I did rescue you, didn't I?'

'Don't rub it in,' said Alfie.'

Peggy thought for a moment before she agreed to the plan. 'There's one problem. I don't know where the police house is.'

'I do,' said Alfie. 'I deliver milk to him. Go back to the lane, follow it until you get to the crossroads, turn to the right and it's the house on the corner, there's a sign on the door.'

'Okay, I'll find it,' said Peggy.

Alfie held out his hand and Peggy shook it. 'Good luck,' he said firmly.

Peggy leaned forward and kissed him on the cheek. 'Good luck to you too. 'Don't let him catch you.'

Alfie blushed. 'I'll head for the den,' he whispered. 'He'll never find me there.'

Alfie got to this hands and knees like a sprinter ready to start a race. He looked back at Peggy and winked, then he gritted his teeth, took four deep breaths and began to count.

'3, 2, 1. GO!'

Alfie sprang out from the bushes with a yell and raced up the hill. Peggy held her breath and crossed her fingers as she heard William Travers shout at Alfie as he ran past her hiding place.

'Hey, you, come back here...Just you wait until I get hold of you...'

Peggy waited until William's calls had faded into the distance before she crawled out of her hiding place and headed back to the lane. She took a quick look around before stepping out from the cover of the trees, then she began to run.

'I'm bringing help, Mrs Henderson. Hang on in there,' she muttered to herself.

At the crossroads, Peggy turned right, and just as Alfie had promised there was a house on the corner with a sign on the door that said, *'Police.'*

Peggy hammered on the door with her fist and rattled the knocker at the same time. PC Watson threw the door open and glared out into the night.

'Who's making that racket? I'm trying to write my reports in here.'

'It's me, Peggy Larkin.'

'So it is. What can I do for you, Peggy Larkin? Have you found another German spy?'

Peggy blurted out the whole story in one breath.

'It's Mrs Henderson. She's collapsed and William Travers is chasing Alfie, he broke in and tied them up, I rescued Alfie but I couldn't rescue Mrs Henderson, you have to come now she needs the doctor or she'll die.'

'Whoa, slow down, girl,' said the policeman. 'Now, what's this about Beryl?'

As Peggy told her story again, PC Watson grabbed his coat and fastened his truncheon to his belt. He called to his two brothers to help.

'Eric, John, get your boots on, there's a criminal on the loose.' He turned back to Peggy and crouched down next to her. 'Where has young Alfie gone, do you know?'

'He's going to hide in his den by the river,' said Peggy. 'I don't think William will be able to find him if he gets there, but he might catch him before he does.'

'Where exactly is this den?' asked PC Watson.

'There's a small plank bridge near where the stream meets the river,' said Peggy. It's just up from there. Please hurry.'

PC Watson turned to his bothers. 'Eric, John, you heard the young lady. Get yourself up there now and see if you can find him. I'm going to Beryl Henderson's house.'

'What shall I do?' asked Peggy.

'You wait here for Doctor Harris. I'm going to give him a call now. He'll know what medication Beryl needs.'

Eric and John raced over to the woods while PC Watson got his bike from the shed and pedalled off to Mrs Henderson's. Peggy waited by the gate and a few minutes later a car pulled up. A man leaned out of the driver's window and called to her.

'Come on, no time to waste, jump in.'

Peggy had never been in a car before. Dr Harris smiled at her as she climbed into the front seat.

'I hear you've got yourself involved in a bit of an adventure,' he said.

'I'd rather not be in one,' said Peggy. 'I'd rather things go back to being nice and quiet. Will Mrs Henderson be all right?'

Doctor Harris frowned. 'I hope so, it depends how long she's been unconscious. It sounds like Hypoglycaemia to me.'

Peggy nodded. 'That sounds like what she said to Alfie before she collapsed. She needs her medicine.'

'She doesn't need her medicine. That could kill her. What she needs is some glucose to get her blood sugar levels up. I can fix that.'

Doctor Harris drove to the crossroads, then turned towards the big house. Peggy crossed her fingers and prayed they would be in time.

The doctor pulled up on the lane outside Mrs Henderson's, grabbed his bag and leapt from the car leaving the engine running and the door open. Peggy got out and ran after him.

PC Watson's bike was lying on the floor near the front door. Peggy stepped round it and ran up to Mrs Henderson's bedroom. The policeman had untied Mrs Henderson and carried her over to her bed. As Peggy ran in, the doctor was about to check her pulse.

'Right, leave this to me. I think we're in time,' he said.

PC Watson let go of Mrs Henderson's hand and gently stroked her hair. 'Come back to us, Beryl.'

Peggy stood by the bedside and asked if there was anything she could do. The doctor gave her some instructions.

'Go to the kitchen and make some tea, the sweeter the better. Don't worry about it being hot. If you can find a couple of biscuits, bring them with you.'

Peggy ran down to the kitchen and picked up the teapot. It was still warm. William had obviously made himself a drink. Peggy put four teaspoons of sugar into the cup and poured the tea into it before pulling the biscuit tin out of the cupboard. Mrs Henderson had said biscuits were for special occasions.

'If this isn't a special occasion I don't know what is,' thought Peggy.

She put three of the biscuits on a tray with the tea and carried it carefully upstairs. When she walked into the bedroom Mrs Henderson was awake, propped up on the pillows. She looked at Peggy and smiled weakly.

'Thank you, Margaret, it seems you have saved the day.'

Peggy placed the tea tray on the bedside cabinet and gave Mrs Henderson a hug.

'I'm sorry for what I did, I know it was wrong.'

Mrs Henderson stroked Peggy's hair and smiled softly. 'Don't worry about it now, dear. I've had time to think about that. It's high time I stopped living in the past.'

Mrs Henderson smiled at Peggy, then at the policeman. PC Watson squeezed her hand and got to his feet. 'Right, it's time I did my duty, we have a villain on the loose. Where did you say this den was, Peggy?'

Peggy gave the constable directions and followed him to the door. Before she had the chance to walk through she was stopped by the doctor.

'Peggy, stay here please. I need to have a look at you too.'

'Why? I feel fine,' said Peggy.

'Which train did you arrive on?' asked the doctor.

'Train three,' said Peggy. 'But I was on train four for a short time too.'

Then I really will have to examine you, Peggy,' said the doctor. 'It seems that some of the children on train three brought Scarlet Fever with them from London. It has spread so fast that all the isolation wards in the area are full. We need to make sure you haven't caught it too.'

Peggy realised that she had been feeling a little hot all evening but she had put it down to the excitement of running from William Travers. She wanted the doctor to examine her, just in case, but she was more concerned for Alfie.

'Come over here, Peggy,' said Doctor Harris.

Peggy turned and ran for the door. 'Sorry, I have to make sure Alfie is all right first. I'll come back later.'

Doctor Harris rushed to the bedroom door but Peggy was already half way down the stairs. She ran out of the front door and turned down the lane towards Brown's farm. A hundred yards later she pushed through the gap in the hedge and entered the wood.

CHAPTER EIGHTEEN

Peggy headed straight for the stream and ran through it without taking off her shoes and socks. She ran down the other side of the hill and took the plank bridge without even thinking about the gaps. When she reached the riverbank she stopped and listened for a while. In the distance she could see the flash of torches and the sound of men calling to each other. The Watson brothers were still on the trail.

Peggy sat on the path to get her breath back. She had begun to feel a little light headed and her throat felt sore and dry. She wished she had taken a drink before leaving Mrs Henderson's house, but there hadn't been time.

Peggy got unsteadily to her feet and walked down the path towards the den. The moonlight filtered down through the trees and cast long shadows on the floor. Peggy walked on until the old willow came into sight, then she stopped to get her breath back again.

As she approached the den she began to feel a little dizzy. Peggy leaned against the tree and closed her eyes for a moment. When she opened them, William Travers was standing in front of her.

'What have we here?' he growled. 'She should be tucked up in bed at this time of night. She didn't ought to be out in a dangerous wood.'

Peggy swayed and backed against the tree to keep her balance. 'Where's Alfie?' she croaked.

'Alfie? What do you know about Alfie,' said William. He's the young pup I've been chasing...'

He was silent for a moment as he put the pieces of the puzzle together. 'Now I see it!' he exclaimed. 'You helped him escape. It wasn't my knots at all. Well now, seeing as you are the reason I had to skip dinner, you can pay his forfeit for him.'

William took a step forward and raised his hands. Peggy ducked under his arm and stood with her back to the river. William turned to face her. His eyes became narrower than ever and a cruel grin spread over his face.

'I'll teach y...'

Suddenly the door of the den flew open and Alfie stepped onto the path holding the forked stick he used as a door prop. As William turned he jabbed him in the back and pushed as hard as he could. William lost his balance and hit the water with a loud splash.

Alfie gave Peggy a concerned look. 'Are you all right?'

Peggy nodded. 'Yes, he didn't' hurt, me. I was wondering where you were.'

Alfie grinned. 'I got here a good five minutes before he did. I heard him puffing and panting from a hundred yards away. I saw him hide behind the willow to ambush me. He didn't have a clue I was only a couple of feet away.'

William began to flounder in the water. He went under twice, then resurfaced and waved his arms.

'I can't swim,' he spluttered. 'Help me, I'm drowning.'

'Give me one good reason why I should help you, William Travers?' said Alfie.

'I'm sorry for everything,' said William. 'Help me get out.'

'What do you think, Peggy?' asked Alfie.

'I don't trust him.'

'Nor do I,' said Alfie. 'But we can't leave him to drown.'

Alfie ran back to his den and brought out a length of rope from his case. He looped it around the trunk of the willow and stood on the riverbank with one end of the rope in his hand. He threw the other end towards William.

'Catch hold of that, William. I'll keep the tension on the rope at this end while you pull yourself towards the shallows, but if you come too close, or try to climb out, I'll let it go and you'll end up back where you were. I won't throw it to you a second time.'

William spluttered something and grabbed the rope. Alfie dug in his heels and pulled tight on his end of the rope allowing the tree to take the strain while William pulled himself back towards the bank. When his feet found the safety of the riverbed Alfie told him to stop. William obeyed and stood in the river as the water lapped under his chin.

'I'm getting cold in here,' he said. 'I'll catch my death if I don't get out soon. Let me out. I promise not to hurt you.'

'You're just fine where you are,' replied Alfie. He didn't trust William to keep to his word.

Peggy sat down on the riverbank and let her head fall to her chest. She felt very tired all of a sudden.

A few minutes later they heard the calls of the Watson brothers and saw the flash of torch lights. Alfie shouted to attract their attention.

'Over here, we've caught him.'

PC Watson was the first to arrive. He took the rope from Alfie and tied it off round the willow. He shone his torch into the face of William Travers and told him to pull himself out.

By the time his brothers arrived, PC Watson had arrested William and placed him in handcuffs. He sat with his back to the willow tree and proclaimed his innocence.

'What am I being charged with? I've done nothing.'

'Breaking and entering, kidnap, attempted kidnap... I think we've got enough on you to keep you in prison for many a year, William,' said PC Watson. 'I hope you get an extra five years for leaving Beryl alone when she told you she was about to collapse.'

Eric and John dragged William to his feet and marched him off along the path. PC Watson turned to Peggy and Alfie with a smile. 'I have to say, what a wonderful job you have done here. To catch a man like William Travers takes a lot of nerve. You ought to become a policeman when you grow up, young Alfie.'

Alfie went red and stared at his shoes.

As for you, Peggy Larkin. I really can't thank you enough. Beryl means the world to me, I don't know what I'd have done if anything had happened to her. You should feel really proud of yourself. I'm going to see to it that the pair of you get a special commendation from the police. Now, I'd better catch up with Eric and John I want to have a nice long chat with William. I take it you can find your own way home from here.'

PC Watson walked quickly after his brothers, leaving Peggy and Alfie at the side of the river. Peggy had begun to shiver so Alfie gave her his jumper to wear.

'You look really ill, Peggy. Come on, I'll take you home.'

Peggy leaned against Alfie and they left the woods together. Alfie carried Peggy on piggyback across the plank bridge and the stream. It took them almost forty minutes to get back to the house.

Doctor Harris rushed to meet them as Alfie staggered up the lane with Peggy on his back. He lifted her in his arms and carried her into the house. Mrs Henderson had recovered and sat in the kitchen drinking tea. She hurried out as the doctor carried Peggy into the hallway.

'Put her in my room. It's the nearest. Oh dear, Peggy, you do look ill. Hang on sweetheart we'll soon get you well again.'

Alfie paced up and down outside the bedroom as Doctor Harris and Mrs Henderson got Peggy into a nightgown and tucked up in bed. When Mrs Henderson emerged a few minutes later she told Alfie he had better go home.

'There's nothing you can do here, Alfie, she's in good hands. Go and get some rest, I'll keep you informed as to how she's doing.'

Alfie walked slowly down the stairs and made his way to the front door. 'She will be all right won't she? She's my best friend now.'

Mrs Henderson put her arm around Alfie's shoulders. 'I know, Alfie, I think the world of her too. It's strange isn't it? She's only been here a few days and she's already become a big part of our lives.'

'I've had Scarlet Fever, can I visit?' asked Alfie.

'Come whenever you like, Alfie. You can sit with her for a while every day if you want to. She has to stay here, there's no room at the hospital.'

Alfie opened the front door to let himself out, then turned back to Mrs Henderson. 'Sorry about picking the lock the other day. I wouldn't have done it if I had known why the room was locked.'

Mrs Henderson smiled sadly. It doesn't matter now, Alfie. The past is the past. Let's all concentrate on making sure young Margaret gets well. This house has seen enough of sick children.'

Alfie closed the door behind him and walked slowly back to the farm with his fingers firmly crossed.

CHAPTER NINETEEN

Over the next four days Peggy drifted in and out of fitful sleep. As the fever took hold she began to have the strangest dreams. At times it seemed as though she was back at home in London with her mum and dad, but she always seemed to be looking at them from the outside of the room. Sometimes the dreams were more menacing and she found herself face to face with William Travers again. In between the dreams she would wake for a few minutes but before long she was asleep again as her sick body tried to heal itself.

At times, as she lay half asleep with her temperature raging, she imagined that Alfie was sat at her bedside talking to her about the things they might do when she was well enough. At other times it was Doctor Harris. He made her swallow some strange tasting medicine that he fed to her on a spoon. Mostly though, it was Mrs Henderson. She always seemed to be at the bedside whenever Peggy woke. Peggy could hear her voice in her dreams, soothing her, telling her that everything was going to be all right.

'You get well now, Margaret Larkin, don't you dare fade like my Katie. Be strong, fight it.'

*****

After five days the fever broke and Peggy woke with the sun shining through the window and her mother sat at her bedside holding her hand.

'MUM! cried Peggy. 'What are you doing here?'

'I'm here to be with you, silly. I only arrived last night. I'm sorry I didn't get here sooner, darling. Mrs Henderson sent me a telegram but I've been away on a course to learn how to use some new machinery and I didn't get home until yesterday. The local police brought a message round. Mrs Henderson had been calling them every day. I jumped on the train as soon as I could.'

'It's all right, Mum. Don't be sorry,' said Peggy.

Mrs Larkin smiled and brushed the hair from Peggy's forehead. 'Thank goodness your fever has broken at last. Mrs Henderson has been nursing you day and night for five days solid. She must be exhausted.'

Peggy tried to sit up in bed but Mrs Larkin told her to get some more rest. 'There's plenty of time to talk when you're feeling stronger.'

Peggy lay back and closed her eyes. 'How's Alfie? He saved me twice from William Travers, you know?'

'I've heard all about it,' said Mrs Larkin. 'He's a very brave boy, although when he tells the story, you seem to be the hero of it. He's been to see you every day while you've been ill. He'll be here again this afternoon no doubt. I'll send him in for five minutes if you're awake.'

Peggy smiled and drifted back to sleep. When she woke again both Mrs Larkin and Mrs Henderson were sat by her bed. Mrs Henderson fed her some broth while Mrs Larkin gave her the latest news from London. She also told her about Harry. He had ended up with a wonderful family and was enjoying himself tremendously.

Mrs Larkin reached into her bag and brought out an envelope. 'I've had a letter from Dad, Peggy. He wants you to know he's all right. He sends his love.'

The next morning Peggy felt much better. The red rash had begun to fade and she had her appetite back. Mrs Henderson propped her up on two thick pillows and gave her a breakfast tray with a cup of sweet tea, a boiled egg and a slice of toast cut into soldiers. Peggy tucked in hungrily.

Later in the morning Mrs Larkin sat by Peggy's bed, patted her hand and pulled a sad face. 'I've got to go back today, Peggy. I was only allowed a few days leave. I do important war work now.'

Peggy nodded. 'I understand, Mum.'

Mrs Larkin pulled her chair up closer and held Peggy's hand. 'They are still telling us that the bombing is about to start and I really do feel better knowing you are out of the way of all that, Peggy. But, if you really want to come home, I won't try to persuade you not to. I've missed you terribly, but I was happy knowing you were safe.'

'I've missed you too, Mum, and I've only been away a week or so,' said Peggy. 'I still feel a bit like I'm on holiday. I should have started school this week but I couldn't because I was ill.'

Mrs Henderson let herself into the room and stood at the side of the bed next to Mrs Larkin.

Peggy smiled at her and turned back to her mother. 'What I'm saying is, Mum. I miss you, but I don't want you to worry about me all the time, especially if you're at work and the bombs start to fall. Mrs Henderson looks after me really well and Alfie's here too. I'm happy to stay if Mrs Henderson will have me.'

'Mrs Henderson dabbed her eyes with a handkerchief and swallowed deeply. 'You are welcome to stay with me as long as you like, Peggy Larkin. Both your mother and I were hoping you would decide to stay, but I wasn't very sure you would want to. I was very mean to you the other day.'

'That was my own fault,' said Peggy. She was silent for a moment then a big grin spread across her face. 'You just called me Peggy.'

'Everyone else does,' said Mrs Henderson. 'So I think it's time I did too.'

THE END

Printed in Poland
by Amazon Fulfillment
Poland Sp. z o.o., Wrocław

49033513R00049